I0520476

MAEDEIVA MYRE

Fifty Plastic Bottles and the Shoeshine Box

Mosaic Press

First published by Mosaic Press 2018

Copyright © 2018 by Maedeiva Myre

All rights reserved. No part of this publication may be reproduced, stored or transmitted in any form or by any means, electronic, mechanical, photocopying, recording, scanning, or otherwise without written permission from the publisher. It is illegal to copy this book, post it to a website, or distribute it by any other means without permission.

Designations used by companies to distinguish their products are often claimed as trademarks. All brand names and product names used in this book and on its cover are trade names, service marks, trademarks and registered trademarks of their respective owners. The publishers and the book are not associated with any product or vendor mentioned in this book. None of the companies referenced within the book have endorsed the book.

This novel is entirely a work of fiction. Certain public figures are mentioned, but the characters involved are wholly imaginary. The names, characters, and incidents portrayed are the work of the author's imagination. Any resemblance to actual persons (with the exception of public figures), living or dead, events or localities is entirely coincidental. None of the public figures mentioned in the book have endorsed the book.

Second edition

ISBN: 978-9692324106

This book was professionally typeset on Reedsy.
Find out more at reedsy.com

DEDICATION
To those who endure and survive.

Acknowledgement

Thank you, God (the Universe).

Thank you to all the reviewers who reviewed my work and helped me become a better storyteller. Your support is invaluable.

Thank you, the editors Amy Shelby, Kimberly Love, and Sarah Tyrrell.

And thank YOU if you have decided to read this story.

Prologue

"Grab his legs. Don't let him move!" a factory worker barked, sending small meteoroids of paan saliva into the air, the red spit spraying from his mouth like crimson rain.

"Believe me, I didn't say any such thing," Kareem cried, his eyes wide with desperation and hands raised in a futile attempt to defend himself.

"He's lying! Babu told me he heard him say it! He insulted us," the worker growled, launching a fist at Kareem's face.

The scorching asphalt beneath barbecued him with inexplicable intensity, but the heat was the least of his problems. The factory workers had forced him to the ground, just a few miles from the factory. They surrounded him, their fists clenched and foreheads wrinkled.

"Let's wait for Babu," another worker shouted.

"We're not waiting for Babu. We know enough!" The worker delivered another blow to Kareem's face. Men around them raised their voices in agreement while a few stood still, watching in horror from a distance, fearing that if they intervened, they too could end up on the ground.

His nose bled profusely, dripping all over his shirt. Before he could recover from the previous blow, another fist collided with his jaw, followed by a flurry of blows. Their voices erupted like thunder as they attacked him from all angles, like piranhas feasting on a hapless mackerel.

"Please!" a muffled plea came from his bloodied lips before Kareem fell into stillness.

They left him in a puddle of his own blood.

In the distance, the factory chimney exhaled black smoke, darkening the sky above as if to announce the tragedy.

1

The Dhak Dhak Girl

The men watched transfixed, their eyes glued to the TV screen as if under a spell.

A delicate Maang Tikka adorned her forehead, nestled beneath an embroidered dupatta elegantly secured with a silver hairpin. She wore a shimmery dress with a stunningly embellished blouse that sparkled as she leaped and spun effortlessly.

Her brown eyes, enhanced by a blend of shadows and liners, seemed to beckon as she gazed into the camera, drawing her audience into a trance.

Katib forced his toes into the small holes of the tea shop's weathered wall, using every ounce of his strength to lift his body for a better view. His tiny hands tightly clutched the protruding, uneven bricks, providing support for his straining toes. Sweat trickled down his forehead as he tried to balance himself. Just like the men in the tea shop, he gazed wide-eyed at the flickering TV screen.

Their eyes widened, and a few leaned forward as Madhuri Dixit cast another glance their way, ensnaring their complete attention.

Mushtaq, the owner of Mushtaq's Tea Shop, played famous Madhuri songs for his customers every morning on a VCR. In a place where few people owned a VCR or a television, Mushtaq had a competitive edge over other tea shops that lacked a TV or radio, thanks to his daily Madhuri playlist that repeated the top ten songs from her famous films. He was an excellent salesman; people came for Madhuri, not for the tea.

"Go home, Katib, or I'll tell Bashir," Mushtaq hurled a warning at the boy as he noticed him.

"Every day he's here, useless little brat!" he grumbled while pouring tea into cups for his customers.

Katib immediately detached from the wall and darted toward a narrow alley with a long line of vendors selling everything from food to fairness creams.

He hopped over a regurgitating gutter, humming the Madhuri song he had just heard and memorized when he noticed his neighborhood children playing cricket at the end of the street.

"Oye, Nadir, can I join, please?" he shouted to the team, receiving a resounding 'no' in return from one of the kids.

"We don't have any room for a new player. Stop bothering us!" another child snapped.

"I can be the extra batsman," Katib offered but received nothing but silence.

Katib sat on a shop's stairs to watch the kids play. After the match, he strolled aimlessly through the narrow alleys and looked at Bollywood posters outside movie rental shops until a shopkeeper rebuked him, forcing him to run away.

* * *

As Katib entered the house, he found Rukhsana fixing the loose ropes of the Charpai. With one foot firmly planted on the frame, she pulled one of the loose ropes with all her might.

"Where were you?" she asked.

"I watched Nadir play cricket." Katib sat nearby, avoiding eye contact with his mother.

"Is Nadir playing cricket all day? Where do you disappear to after?" Rukhsana asked.

Katib stayed quiet, biting his fingernails.

"Bashir keeps asking me what you do all day, and I don't know what to tell him. You are almost eight now, Katib. You can't keep wandering about every day," she said as she gave the rope one final tug and wrapped it around the frame before tying it into a knot.

"What do I do then?" Katib said, watching his mother tighten another loose rope.

"Learn how to fix shoes," she said.

"And repair and polish shoes like Chacha?" Katib shook his head in disdain.

"What is wrong with shoe-mending?" Rukhsana halted and looked at her son momentarily before resuming. "It's a great skill. One day, you can have your own shoe repair shop."

"I already told you I want to be like Shahid Afridi, not an ordinary cobbler. Please buy me a cricket kit so I can start practicing." Katib jumped to his feet and pretended to strike an imaginary ball with an imaginary bat as he walked into the bedroom, leaving Rukhsana shaking her head.

At night, on the Charpai, the shimmery dress and the seductive dance moves roamed freely in his imagination before he finally drifted off to sleep.

3

2

Kareem's Debt

A few months after Kareem's death at the factory, a man came to visit Bashir. He was unmistakably a factory worker, his face weathered by years under the sun and hands hardened and roughened with calloused fingertips.

He wasn't part of Kareem's regular circle of friends, all of whom had already visited to offer their condolences. Bashir studied the stranger first from a distance, then from a few feet away, as if proximity could reveal his identity.

Rukhsana prepared lemonade for the guest and asked Bashir to serve him.

"Who is he?" she whispered in Bashir's ear.

"I don't know, or maybe I don't remember." Bashir shook his head.

He approached the man and offered his hand. The man took his hand and shook it gently.

"You probably don't know me," the man said, "I used to work with Kareem in the factory."

"Kareem never mentioned you." Bashir smiled cordially.

"We were not that close," the man admitted awkwardly and

placed his hand on Bashir's shoulder, "I am so sorry about this."

"It's Allah's will." Bashir's voice quivered. He quickly cleared his throat audibly to suppress it and said, "Thank you for coming here today."

"Did you find out what happened?" the man asked.

"No, we don't know," Bashir said. "The factory owner said the workers got offended by something he said."

"I hope you can work through your sorrow," the man said after a moment of silence.

"Thank you," Bashir said with a polite smile in return.

The man scratched his chin with his forefinger, contemplating. Bashir wished he would leave. He offered lemonade to the man, but he refused with a wave of his hand. "No, no, I have a sore throat. Lemon could irritate it."

Bashir placed the glass on the tray and waited for the man to say something so the awkwardness could dissolve.

"This is probably not the right time for this, but I have to do it now," the man spoke after a moment of pause.

"Kareem owed me money," the man continued carefully. "He told me he'd return it next month." The man clasped his hands as he studied Bashir.

"How much money?" Bashir asked with a perplexed look.

"Sixty-five thousand rupees. All in cash."

Bashir, speechless, stood frozen, unaware that he was staring hard at the man and making him uncomfortable.

"Sixty-five thousand?" Bashir let out a nervous laugh.

"Yes. All in cash," the man repeated with a polite smile.

Bashir scoffed incredulously. "Why would he take such a big amount and not tell us?"

The man did not like the suspicion in Bashir's tone. His face turned grave, and the polite smile slowly shrunk into pursed lips.

"If you don't believe me, you can come with me and ask the witness," the man said sternly. He pulled a piece of paper from his pocket, opened it, and smoothed the wrinkles with his fingers before offering it to Bashir. It had the date, time, and amount written in numbers. Bashir looked at it and immediately recognized Kareem's messy handwriting.

"His name is Syed Awan. If this is not enough proof, you can ask him. We had an agreement." The man pointed at the paper in Bashir's hand.

Bashir looked up to meet his gaze before lowering it back to the paper.

"Why would my brother borrow this much money?" He shook his head in disbelief.

"He told me he wanted to buy a rickshaw." The man shrugged. "Look, you seem like a decent man. Kareem was a good man. I don't want to involve the police to get my money," the man cautioned.

Bashir looked at the paper again, then raised his head and forced a smile.

* * *

"He thought a rickshaw would be a good option for a side income," Rukhsana explained.

"Okay, so where is the rickshaw?" Bashir demanded with his hands on his hips.

"I don't know." Her voice trembled.

"If there's no rickshaw, then where is the money?" Bashir

barked.

Rukhsana remained silent, offering no response.

Bashir took his anger out on the water bucket in his way as he stormed out of the house, muttering to himself.

Rukhsana stayed up all night hunting for the money in all the hiding spots she knew of in the house without any success. She looked twice in the same corner as if the money would magically appear the second time. Her heart throbbed like a hammer into a wall as she searched desperately.

3

Bashir's Shoe Repair Shop

"Do you know how much is sixty-five thousand?" Bashir asked.

"Chacha, I don't know," Katib said.

Katib, who had come to deliver lunch, usually left right after. However, today, Bashir asked him to stay. He instructed the boy to sit on a small stool in the shop's corner while he stood nearby, examining a broken sandal.

"How much is five hundred?" Bashir crossed his arms over his chest as he fixed his gaze on Katib, watching him squirm under pressure.

Katib considered before he answered, "Fifty and fifty."

Bashir glared at the boy, "Fifty and fifty make one hundred!"

Katib counted on his fingers and looked up to see if Bashir had gone back to the sandal, but his uncle was looking right at him, expecting a quick answer.

"Chacha, I don't know," Katib mumbled, deliberately averting his eyes from Bashir, keeping his head lowered.

"If fifty and fifty make a hundred, how many hundreds make five hundred?"

"Five?" Katib blurted out so Bashir could at least turn his gaze away.

"Shabash!" exclaimed Bashir, bolstering Katib's confidence with a hearty pat on the back. Katib straightened up, spine erect, head high, ready to look Bashir in the eye.

"Now, how many hundreds make a thousand?" Bashir asked, his eyes glistening with expectation. Katib looked away into the distance while he counted on his fingers.

"Ten?" he took a shot.

"Shabash!"

"Now, how many thousands make ten thousand?"

"Twenty!" he shouted, rising from the stool. Bashir sighed as he sat down on the floor mat with the broken sandal.

"Try again," he said, opening the needle box. The spark of confidence that had ignited in Katib quickly faded. He shrunk into a crouched position on the stool, wrapping his arms around his knees, his spine arched like a rainbow.

Bashir pinned a nail on the sandal to fix its strap as he glanced at Katib, who calculated on his fingers. He let the boy take all the time he needed.

"Chacha, I don't know," the boy said after a moment.

"Ten," Bashir assisted. "Now tell me, how many thousands make fifty thousand?"

"Five?" Katib looked at Bashir, unsure.

Bashir shook his head. "The answer is in the question," he said.

"Fifty?" Katib changed the answer.

"Shabash!"

"And how many thousands make sixty thousand?"

"Sixty?"

"Yes! And Sixty-five thousand?"

Katib calculated for a moment. "Sixty-and-five?" he answered hesitantly.

Bashir studied him for a moment. Katib wasn't sure if he got it right.

"This is how much money we owe somebody," Bashir said. "Do you understand how much money that is?"

"A lot of hundreds," Katib said.

"Yes, a lot. I can't do it myself. Would you help me?" he asked.

"Yes, Chacha."

"Shabash!" Bashir said before lowering his gaze back to the sandal. "You are a big boy now, Katib. It's time you learn to take responsibility."

Katib wasn't sure how he was supposed to help or take responsibility. *I hope he doesn't want me to mend shoes.* Katib thought as he walked back home.

4

The Factory

"If you don't want to mend shoes, then you'll have to learn factory work," Rukhsana said while washing dishes with dirt. She placed a handful on a dirty steel plate and worked it around thoroughly with her hand until it picked up food particles. Afterward, she rinsed the plate under tap water and placed it to dry on a cement table next to the tap.

"I know nothing about it!" Katib exclaimed, playing with his infant sister, Kanji, on the Charpai.

"That's why I said learn it." She looked at him sharply, rinsing another steel plate. "On Monday, you have a job interview. I don't want to hear anything; you are going!"

Katib frowned at the idea but refrained from starting another argument. *At least, factory work is better than mending shoes.* He found comfort in the thought.

Rukhsana had no say in household matters; Kareem always made all the decisions. When he passed away, the responsibility shifted to Bashir—a change that deeply concerned Rukhsana.

"So what if Kareem isn't here; it is your home, too." Her mother's voice crackled through the receiver of an old Nokia phone with a faded matte plastic casing adorned with scratches and marks.

"If he says anything, tell him the house belongs to you and Kareem's children," her mother continued.

Rukhsana adjusted Kanji on her other hip while listening to her mother and contemplating her family's future.

"But ma, even if Bashir doesn't object, other people will. People will frown upon me living with my brother-in-law. And one day, he's going to have his own family," Rukhsana said, her eyebrows curling with worry.

"Let people say what they want to!" her mother barked, worry and anger mingling in her voice. "Rukhsana, we cannot take the burden of three more people. That is your home with or without Kareem," her mother concluded their call, causing Rukhsana's eyebrows to furrow even more.

On the interview day, Rukhsana was up early, way before the Fajr prayer. She prepared breakfast for Katib and Bashir, then helped Katib dress up for the factory interview.

"Just be a good boy and learn the factory work," she told him as she combed his hair before a broken mirror reclined against the bedroom's weather-beaten wall.

"If you don't get a job, your Chacha will ask us to move out. And where will we go? Tell them you are a fast learner and will do anything, okay?"

Katib nodded as he rubbed the sleep out of his eyes.

* * *

"Tell them you can clean, make tea, and serve guests. Employers need to know your capabilities," Bashir instructed the boy as they rushed to the main road to catch an early bus.

"It will change your life forever if you get this job. You understand?" Bashir said. Katib responded with a nod.

"Now tell me how to make tea as if you are explaining to the recruiter," Bashir asked.

"First, I put water in a pan," Katib began.

"How much water would you add?"

"For three cups, I add four and a half cups of water."

"Shabash. Next?"

"I add patti."

"How many teaspoons of patti?"

"Two full teaspoons if three cups, and two-and-a-half teaspoons if I make four cups."

"Shabash! What would you do next?"

"After the water and the patti boil, I add milk and let it boil for two more minutes," Katib finished.

"Good." Bashir patted the boy's shoulder.

"What if they don't like me?" Katib remarked nervously, his fingernails bearing the brunt of his anxiety.

"Nonsense, your father died working for them, Katib. They owe you this job. Remember to tell them all the things you can do. They might say you are too short, but tell them you can stand on a stool and perform all kinds of tasks," Bashir said, ushering Katib toward the approaching bus.

As soon as the bus stopped, the passengers rushed to it like moths to a flame. The driver's assistant called people to board the bus for specific destinations: "Gawalmandi, Anarkali, Lohari, come, hurry up. Gawalmandi, Anarkali, Lohari, come quickly."

Bashir helped Katib up and squeezed him in through the jam-packed space.

Once there was no more room, the assistant closed the door, signaling to the approaching passengers that the bus was full.

Katib managed to grab the pole and secure a spot. He tried to wave at Bashir from the window, but the passengers, pressed against one another, completely obscured it. As the bus went over a road bump, its movement caused people to crash into each other. Luckily, Katib couldn't feel anything; the pressure from the surrounding bodies had diminished any sense of movement.

In a short while, the bus halted at a stop. A woman in a veil left her seat, triggering a contest among the other passengers: She pushed toward the door while the passengers rushed to vie for the empty spot. A man standing near the seat won with a fat grin while the woman got off the bus. Katib had to travel clinging to the pole.

The factory stood alone, surrounded by patches of dead grass and a few under-watered Shisham trees with wilted leaves, browned at the edges. Its once-red bricks had faded to a tired, mottled brown. As Katib approached the front gate, the smell of burning coal reached his nostrils, forcing him to wrinkle his nose. He could hear the faint, rhythmic clang of machinery interspersed with the shouts of workers.

A middle-aged, hefty man sat on a plastic chair with a thick notebook before him on a table to jot down candidates' names. There was a long line of candidates before him. Katib stood at the far end of the line. As he waited for his turn, he observed a little girl in the distance, carefully placing freshly molded bricks in rows across the drying yard. Strands of her messy, unkempt hair glued to her forehead, cheeks, and chin. The sticky sweat made her entire face glisten, but she seemed unbothered.

"Do you work here?" a voice said.

Katib turned to find a teenage boy in a pale blue Shalwar Kameez, ironed to perfection. He was tall enough to clean ceiling fans without a stool.

"No," Katib replied, shifting his gaze back to the girl. "I am here for work."

"Are you here by yourself?" The boy followed Katib's gaze and studied the girl.

"Yes," Katib answered.

The boy momentarily glanced back at Katib before adjusting his gaze somewhere else.

"Are you alone here, too?" Katib asked.

The boy nodded. "My father used to be the staff manager here," he said, scratching his chin reflectively, gazing into the distance.

"Do you think they'll hire us?" Katib looked at the boy.

"I don't know about you." The boy shrugged, then turned to Katib, studying him. "What can you do? Do you know how to use the factory equipment?"

Katib contemplated, then replied: "I can make tea and clean."

"That's it?" The boy laughed. "My father has taught me how to use the machines, clean them, and even fix them. I know a lot of stuff. I am sure they can't turn me down. You should at least know how to run a machine," he remarked.

"I can't run a machine, but I am good at cleaning," Katib said.

The boy laughed again. "There are millions like you who can clean. You think they'll hire you because you can clean?"

"I can also make tea. I am very good at it. Ask my mother!" Katib asserted.

"I can make tea as well," the boy remarked. "Look at all these people." The boy pointed at the men standing in the line. "Look

15

at them closely. They are rugged, built for factory work, have experience, and probably have references. Do you think they'll prefer you over them?"

Katib glanced at the men in the line. The boy was right; Katib was the only kid there.

"I really need this job." Katib turned to the boy, his eyebrows curled to the extreme. "Can you help me?"

"How can I help you? I can't make you taller!" The boy turned away. "Just relax. Maybe they can use you in some way."

Katib looked back at the long line of rugged candidates and sighed.

As the line moved forward, Katib stole a glance at the recruiter: his bushy mustache, muscular frame, and crooked teeth did little to inspire confidence.

"Next!" the recruiter called out.

Katib and the boy waited in line as the recruiter spoke to candidates, taking down their information for administrative work. Katib heard the recruiter ask a man about his CNIC. Not knowing what it referred to, he immediately tugged on the boy's arm.

"What is a CNIC?" he asked, worried.

"Don't worry; you won't need it," the boy replied dismissively.

"How can I impress him?" Katib asked as he studied the recruiter.

"Just tell him you know how to operate the machines," the boy said. "Once you get in, you will learn."

"I am worried he'll ask difficult questions about the machines. And I know nothing about them. Wait, I know how to ride a bicycle. Do you think that could help?"

The boy threw a glance at Katib and then shook his head. "Are you serious? It is a construction factory. They don't need kids who can ride bikes."

"I can fetch newspaper on a bicycle!"

"Stop being an idiot! Don't mention that," the boy warned.

"Then what do I say if he asks questions about machinery?"

"Tell him, Sahib, give me a task. You need to watch me do it to know I can. Usually, they don't have time for questions." The boy turned away and waited for his turn.

"But what if he gave me a task?"

"I don't think he would. Just be confident and stop bothering me." The boy moved forward and pulled out his cell phone, hoping to be left alone.

'*Sahib, you need to watch me do it to know I can,*' Katib rehearsed under his breath. '*I know machines, Sahib. Please, give me a chance.*'

When it was the teenage boy's turn, the recruiter asked standard questions before nodding at him. The boy winked at Katib as he exited the line with a fat grin.

Katib moved forward and waited with his hands clasped. The recruiter looked him over and studied his petite frame before lowering his gaze to the thick notebook where he scribbled the candidates' information.

"What's your name? Any references?" the recruiter asked.

"My name is Katib Ali Kareem, Sahib. My father died in the accident." Katib had practiced this line with Bashir earlier. He delivered it with mastery, eliciting the expected reaction: the recruiter looked up urgently.

"Oh," he said, "I am sorry about your father." He gave Katib another quick, investigative look before lowering his gaze to his notebook. "Did someone come with you?"

"No, Sahib," Katib said and then quickly explained his worth

17

for the factory. "Sahib, I can cook and clean very well."

"We already have a boy for cooking and cleaning, and you are too young for any open jobs," the recruiter said, dismissing him politely.

"But Sahib, I can cook well. I can make tea. As many cups as you want. I can clean floors, shelves, even fans; I can stand on a stool to clean ceiling fans."

"We already have a boy for cleaning," the recruiter repeated firmly.

"But Sahib, I know a lot about factory equipment, too," Katib said confidently, as advised by the teenage boy.

"Really? You know machines and tools?" the recruiter asked, raising his eyebrows in surprise at the unexpected claim from a child.

Katib nodded.

"Okay. Tell me something, what are pliers?" The recruiter crossed his arms over his chest, waiting for a response.

Katib thought, then said hesitantly: "Sahib, you need to watch me do it to know I can."

5

Rahim's Workshop

All day, Bashir asked questions and muttered things under his breath: *Did you tell him you can make tea? Did you tell him you can stand on a stool to clean fans? Did you mention your father died at his factory? Of course, you didn't tell him everything, or he would have hired you! You can't do anything right. It was such a good opportunity!*

After a few days, Bashir led Katib to an automotive repair shop nestled in a narrow alley near their house. The shop buzzed with the sounds of clanking tools and engines sputtering to life while the smell of oil and grease hung in the air. Inside, a dozen children from the neighborhood toiled away under the watchful gaze of the shop owner.

Rahim, a thirty-something repair shop owner, resembled Yosemite Sam with his large handlebar mustache. His appearance had an uncanny ability to instill fear in children. The scarred skin, long fingernails, and perpetual frown gave him a distinctly villainous aura. His long, dark hair, always perfectly slicked back, added to his menacing look.

"Is he a quick learner?" Rahim asked, using his thumb

and forefinger to wipe away the saliva from the corners of his mouth. When he opened his mouth to speak, Katib could see the permanent tobacco stains on his teeth, which made him look scarier.

"Yes, Rahim, brother. He wants to learn. I promise he will not disappoint you," Bashir pressed.

Rahim scrutinized Katib from head to toe, much like the recruiter, before uttering a thoughtful "hmm" in response.

"Okay," he remarked, wiping the edge of his mouth with his thumb again. "I will pay him ten rupees only," he paused and then continued, "Once he learns and develops certain skills, he'll get the regular amount."

"Oh, Rahim, brother, may Allah give you prosperity and health." Bashir praised the owner and offered his hand to shake, but Rahim turned away and dismissively raised his right hand as he headed toward his young protégés who worked on the engine of a Honda.

"Make sure he is here tomorrow at six sharp," he said.

* * *

Rahim had strict policies for the boys. Once he trained them in automotive repair, they were bound to work exclusively for him unless he decided to let them go.

"Well, I spend a lot of time training them. I reserve the right to use their services for however long I want. They would be nothing without my training." Rahim would tell parents who dared question his ways.

If the children tried to quit Rahim's work, no other shop in the area where Rahim had his connections would hire them. Once one was in a deal with Rahim, there was no way out.

"I don't care how threatening he seems. It is very kind of him to give you work," Rukhsana said as she combed Katib's hair before the broken mirror. "Promise me, you will learn the work with all your heart," she asked firmly, to which Katib responded with a big nod. She hugged him tightly before letting him out of her sight.

* * *

Bashir and Katib arrived at Rahim's workshop before six. The shop was still closed.

"Don't do anything stupid," Bashir said as he left Katib outside the shop. "Just do as he asks."

Katib agreed with a nod and watched Bashir disappear around the corner. He then sat on a metal bench outside the shop as he waited, swinging his legs and biting his fingernails. He hated every minute of it. No more Madhuri, no more wandering, and no more cricket.

Rahim had seventeen children working for him. The children joined him every morning promptly at 6:00 A.M. Those who did not comply with the time lost five rupees from their daily wages. Rahim arrived at the shop precisely at 6:00 A.M. He was never late. A minute past six would earn the latecomer a stinging slap on the back, leaving a reddish imprint of Rahim's chubby hand, in addition to losing the five rupees.

Experienced children skilled in advanced automotive repairs, such as engine replacement, earned over sixty rupees. Conversely, those who handled simpler tasks like changing tires or washing cars received around twenty rupees. The experienced children were responsible for teaching newcomers.

"All the children call me Ustad; you will call me Ustad, too, okay?" Rahim told Katib as he started his day at the workshop.

Assigned to Ali, Katib found himself with a slender and talkative 11-year-old who carried himself with superiority, his words often laced with subtle condescension. No one was good enough for him. He referred to other kids with derogatory names: If someone missed a spot while cleaning, he was 'Andha' for life, and if someone was slow to respond, he was 'Kamakal' or 'Jahil' for life. Ali would never use their real names again.

Dip the sponge into the cleaning solution, wring out as much water as possible, and then rub it on the surface," Ali explained as he worked the sponge over the car's roof. "Rub hard, or it won't shine. And most importantly, don't miss spots like Andha." He pointed at a boy in the distance who cleaned the plastic table and chairs with a wet rag.

"Washing cars is not for everybody; if you make too many mistakes, you'll have to clean tables and chairs, too. That Andha doesn't get paid as much as I do."

He finished cleaning the hood of the Honda, then looked at it from a few feet away with a proud grin. "You see the shine?"

Katib acknowledged with a brief yes.

"That's how you wash a car," he said. "You want to make a lot of money?"

Katib nodded vigorously.

"Good, then stay close to me."

Rahim watched Katib closely from his small room as he slurped tea from a dainty teacup chipped in one corner. Katib saw him looking and quickly lowered his gaze.

"Relax, he may appear intimidating, but he's harmless," Ali whispered in Katib's ear.

* * *

While Katib started at the automotive repair shop, Rukhsana scoured the suburban neighborhood for housekeeping work. No one wanted to hire a maid with an infant daughter.

"He doesn't scold much, does he?" Rukhsana asked Katib as they lounged on the Charpai one evening.

"No, but I don't like this work. It's boring," Katib sighed.

"All work is boring, my dear," she assured him, gently caressing his forehead.

"I want to be like Shahid Afridi, ma," he said. "Can I not become a cricketer like him?"

"Sure, you can," she replied, hesitant. Then, after a moment, in an assuring tone accompanied by a smile, "Of course, you can."

Why not? she thought.

6

Rahim's Money Box

One evening, Ali joined Katib on his walk home from the workshop.

Katib, his face still smudged with grease from the day's work, quietly stashed the ten rupees he had earned in his threadbare pocket.

"How will you spend it?" Ali asked, stuffing his own earnings, sixty rupees, into the worn pocket of his ripped jeans.

"I will give them to Ma," Katib replied earnestly.

"You'll give away all your money? You idiot, that's so stupid," Ali scoffed. "Let me show you what you can do with it."

Ali took Katib to the nearest shop, where they bought small packs of choran worth two rupees. He ripped open a choran packet and poured the grayish-black powder on Katib's palm. As Katib's tongue made contact with the choran, his facial muscles contorted drastically, forcing Ali to burst into a joyful chortle.

Katib laughed, too, licking the rest of the choran.

"Spicy, isn't it?" Ali asked. Katib nodded, stretching out his hand for more.

After a moment, Ali leaned in and whispered in Katib's ear,

"You want to know a secret? Ustad has a box where he keeps all his money."

He paused, studied Katib, and then continued, "I know where he keeps the box."

"So?" Katib asked, confused.

"I am telling you because you said you want a lot of money," he said. "Do you or do you not?"

"I do," Katib said in a shaky voice.

"There's probably forty-five thousand rupees in his box." Ali leaned in even closer, savoring the last of his choran before wiping his sticky hands on his jeans.

"Forty-five thousand?" Katib's eyes went wide.

"Imagine how much we could buy with that money," Ali said.

A lot, Katib thought.

"You and I cannot make this much money even if we work for ten years." Ali reached into his pocket and pulled out a five-rupee coin.

"Even if we work overtime, we cannot make this much money." He tossed the coin in the air. Katib's eyes followed it as it came down and landed back in Ali's palm. "In ten years, I will be twenty-two, and maybe I'll make a little more, but it still won't be a lot." He sent it spinning through the air again, its metallic edges catching the light before landing back on his palm, then shot a glance at Katib, a mischievous glint in his eyes. "Do you understand what I am saying?"

Katib affirmed with a nod.

"I am better than you, and I still can't make a lot of money." He tossed the coin skyward once more, catching it effortlessly in his clenched fist. "I can't live like this." He looked at Katib, "Can you?"

Katib shook his head.

"Stay close to me," Ali said as he walked off, tossing and catching the coin.

"I will!" Katib shouted.

How many thousands make forty-five thousand? Many, many hundreds. Katib thought as he watched Ali disappear in the distance.

* * *

After another grueling week of washing cars and wrestling with tires, the children stood before Rahim, their faces and clothes smeared with dirt, awaiting their earnings.

"You boys are getting good," Rahim said, unlocking his money box with a silver key. "Soon, you all will learn to work on the engines."

Ali's gaze tracked Rahim's fingers as he unlocked the box and sifted through hundreds of bills. He exchanged a glance with Katib, their eyes locking on the money passing between Rahim's fingers.

Rahim pulled out sixty rupees for the older, experienced boys and ten rupees for Katib and the two other new boys.

"If you keep working hard, I might increase your wages," he said and paused, pulled out a handkerchief from his pocket, blew his nose in it, pocketed it, and then approached them, handing out the money. "I pay for your commitment and loyalty, not for your work. There are dozens like you I can hire," Rahim said as he concluded the day.

"6:00 A.M. sharp," he reminded. "I will see you tomorrow."

The boys pocketed their money as they filed out of the workshop.

After the children left, Rahim locked his money box before stashing it away in the small room.

Every Friday night, Rahim would visit his friend's shop, next to his workshop, for a quick card game. Ali had been observing him for a long time. He had been around long enough to understand Rahim's Friday night routine.

8:30 P.M. Pack up.

8:55 P.M. Hand out the wages and send the kids home.

9:11 P.M. Wash up.

9: 25 P.M. Close the workshop and play cards.

9:55 P.M. Come back to the workshop to ensure everything is locked.

10:05 P.M. Head home.

Ali noted the time on an old Rolex with a shattered crystal face, which he claimed belonged to his late uncle.

"Can you believe that? He makes over eleven thousand rupees and pays out only one thousand and three hundred. I have asked him so many times to pay me more, but he doesn't listen," he told Katib as they headed home one night. "And I believe if people don't give you what you want, you should just take it! What do you think?"

"I am not sure," Katib stuttered.

"You are not going to make good money by just washing cars," Ali remarked. "But anyway, forget it. I don't think a coward like you could do something courageous. I'll ask Andha. I am sure he could use the money." Ali walked on, leaving Katib in deep thought.

Katib mulled it over, then spoke with a burst of energy, "I am not a coward!"

Ali stopped, turned to Katib, and parted his lips into a grin.

"Okay," he said. "On Friday, we'll find out just how brave you are."

* * *

Katib could barely wait for that Friday.

When the big day finally arrived, Katib woke up early, all jazzed up. Rukhsana noticed the unusual enthusiasm but disregarded it. *He must have made some friends in the workshop.* She thought as she combed his hair and helped him prepare for the day.

"Don't ever tell the other boys," Ali whispered into Katib's ear as they washed a Honda Civic. "We will quietly take the money and go home. No one will ever find out."

"What if someone caught us and asked about the money?" Katib's forehead wrinkled with worry.

"Just tell people my late uncle left it to me. No one will ask about the dead uncle," Ali said. "And don't you ever dare tell anyone!" he warned.

"I will never!" Katib exclaimed with his hand on his heart.

Ali smiled, "Good, you'd only be hurting yourself if you did; just remember that."

* * *

That night, after the kids left the workshop, Katib and Ali hid behind one of the old workshop cars and piles of junk. Ali checked the time on his battered Rolex. At around 9:25, Rahim left the workshop and headed to his friend's shop, where the group waited for him to join.

The boys stealthily entered the workshop, carefully hiding behind the small wall that separated the workshop area from the service road. They tiptoed toward the small room and found the door locked with a set of identical locks. Ali pulled out a safety pin, inserted its point into the keyhole, and directed Katib to stand guard.

Katib intently watched Ali's deft movements with the safety pin, all the while keeping a vigilant eye on their surroundings.

There was a snap, after which the lock opened effortlessly. Ali looked up at Katib, his face breaking into a triumphant smile. He gave Katib a reassuring nod before turning back to the door.

"I am scared," Katib whispered just loud enough for Ali to hear. "What if he comes back for something?"

"Are you a man or a chicken?" Ali remarked as he worked on the second lock.

"I am not a chicken," Katib muttered as he watched Ali plunge the safety pin into the other lock's keyhole.

There was another audible snap. The second lock fell to the ground with a thud. The boys shared a celebratory laugh, their eyes alight with excitement. With hearts pounding and smiles wide, they made their way into the room.

Ali swiftly retrieved the money box from under the wooden table and promptly set about unlocking its padlock.

Katib, once again, took on the role of keeping watch. After a moment, a loud banging reached his ears, prompting him to turn and discover Ali vigorously pounding the money box against the wall.

"What are you doing? He will hear us!" Katib seethed at the sight before him.

"The safety pin isn't working!" Ali said as he kept pounding the box against the wall.

"Stop it!" Katib hissed.

Another loud bang against the wall reduced the padlock into pieces, adding a noticeable dent to the money box.

"There's nothing I can't do." Ali laughed as he opened the box and reached for the pan-stained bills.

The noise caught Rahim and one of his companions' attention; they turned sharply toward the workshop.

"I think he heard us," Katib whispered, visibly frightened.

"Don't worry, brother, we are done here." Ali pulled hundreds of rupees from the money box and stowed them into his pockets. Katib stayed transfixed.

In the opposite shop, Rahim's friend had his ears pricked up. "Are the kids still working?" he asked.

Rahim shook his head in response. "Must be a stray cat sniffing around," he said.

Ali walked to Katib, patted his shoulder, and handed him a few hundred rupee bills.

"There you go," he said gleefully.

"Can I buy a cricket kit with this?" Katib asked, feeling hundreds of rupee notes in his sweaty palm.

"My brother, you can buy a car," Ali exclaimed with a wide grin, giving him an encouraging pat on the back. They tiptoed out of the back room, trying to contain their smiles. Katib pocketed some bills into his tiny shalwar's pocket and started to count the few in his hand when ...

Clank!

He accidentally hit the bucket that contained the surf water, sending it flying across the floor.

The metallic clang of the bucket confirmed Rahim's suspicion, jolting him into action. In an instant, he sprinted towards the shop, the cards held firmly in his clenched hands as he raced forward.

Katib's face lost all color while Ali quickened his pace, wasting no time. He quickly ducked behind one of the repair cars, but Katib was too slow to hide or run away in this little time, and Ali offered no help. Before he could contemplate an escape, Rahim had his neck in his hand.

"What are you doing here!" he barked, his nostrils flaring as he noticed the bills clutched in the boy's tiny fist. It took a second for Rahim's brain cells to register the situation, then half a second for his chubby hand to land on Katib's cheek, and a couple of nanoseconds to whack Katib repeatedly across the same cheek.

Ali, panicked and tense, observed from behind a car before dropping the stolen money on the ground. Heart racing, he dashed away with swift, silent steps, vanishing into a dark alley.

"Who else is with you?" Rahim demanded, his anger palpable.

"Ustad, please—" Katib stammered through shivering lips.

Suddenly, Rahim noticed more money on the ground in the distance, and his eyes narrowed even more.

I am dead! Katib thought as Rahim dragged him by his collar toward his house.

"Son of a bitch! I give you work, I train you, and this is how you repay me?" Rahim muttered until he was pounding on the fractured tin door that could barely take the onslaught. The walls trembled with each blow Rahim delivered to the fragile door, but Katib couldn't hear the noise. The blow of the slaps

31

had knocked out a nerve in his ear, and all he could hear was consistent ringing.

7

The Shoeshine Box

"Open up!" Rahim thundered. Katib stood motionless beside him with his shirt collar still in his grip. The collar's edge pressed against Katib's neck, digging into his skin as Rahim's grip tightened.

Bang! Bang! Bang! Rahim's fist dented the surface of the tin door as he delivered blow after blow, hammering on its fragile existence. A minute later, Bashir emerged at the door, bewildered.

"Rahim, brother, what is the matter?" Bashir immediately freed Katib from Rahim's firm grip.

"I don't need your filthy thief in my workshop!" Rahim barked. "I better not see him around my workshop again, or I am calling the police!"

Rukhsana came running out of the room as she heard the commotion, wrapping her dupatta around herself. Katib ran inside and sought refuge behind his mother's legs.

"What happened?" Rukhsana asked with rising worry after Bashir closed the tin door. He glared at her in response, his cheeks flushing.

Bashir did not yell that night. Instead, he just sifted through wooden junk pieces lying in the corner of the house.

Is he going to beat Katib with the wood? Rukhsana thought as she watched him gather the wooden pieces.

She warmed her dupatta by blowing into it and massaged Katib's cheek. He cried while cradling his sore cheek.

The next day, Bashir was up at five, not his usual routine. He left early without a word or breakfast. Katib stayed home.

"Why did you listen to that kid? I don't know what to do with you!" Rukhsana muttered as she prepared food on the gas stove. Katib rested on the Charpai, watching Kanji dig her fingers into the gaps of the brick floor, exploring the mud between and its minuscule dwellers. He felt relieved that he no longer had to work for Rahim; however, a sense of tremendous remorse and failure made him bite his fingernails a little too aggressively.

"If Bashir asks you to repair shoes with him, you do it quietly. You understand me?" Rukhsana spoke sharply, then muttered something under her breath that Katib couldn't hear.

I'm not mending shoes. Katib thought and hoped Bashir would forget about work so he could go back to watching Madhuri.

* * *

7:45 A.M.

Later that day, Bashir took Katib to his shoe repair shop. The wooden pieces he had collected earlier had been transformed into a sturdy shoeshine box, meticulously crafted with smooth,

34

polished edges and a lid secured with a brass latch. A rich, earthy scent wafted from the box's freshly oiled surface, mingling with the aroma of leather and polish that permeated the workshop.

"I don't want to force you into mending shoes," Bashir said, his voice gentle but firm. He hammered the nails into the leather strap with practiced precision, each strike echoing softly in the small, cluttered workshop. The nails pierced the strap, securing it to the wooden box. "But you are making things very difficult. You need to learn a skill, and I am only trying to help you."

Katib sat on the shop's stool, watching two ants carry a grain of rice over their heads.

"You are my brother's blood; you are my blood," he said as he made meticulous adjustments to the leather strap, expertly aligning it to the wooden box.

"There's nothing more important to me than my family." With care, he arranged an assortment of shoe polishes and a few well-worn shoe brushes into the shoeshine box

Katib gently tapped his foot near the ants, making them drop the rice and run around in panic. He laughed softly as the little creatures disappeared into a crack in the concrete.

Bashir heard the laugh and shot an angered glance at the boy, studying him. His tense stare compelled the boy to sit up straight, his posture stiffening with unease.

"Do you know how much it cost me?" Bashir asked. "Two hundred and eighty rupees," he answered his own question. "The leather strap alone was one hundred rupees. Nobody spends a dime on somebody unless they care. I spent this money because I care about you. I am trying to teach you something." He glanced at the boy momentarily, making sure he was paying attention.

"You are not a baby anymore. It's time to take control of your life; make yourself useful. Do you understand?" Bashir asked.

Katib gave a big nod, even though he didn't quite understand. In the depths of his mind, thoughts of Madhuri refused to fade away—the maang tikka, the shimmering dress, and the allure of her eyes.

"Only come back when you have earned a hundred rupees," Bashir instructed. "You charge fifteen rupees per shoe shine. Don't take less. If somebody isn't willing to give, serve another customer."

Bashir handed a ten-rupee bill to Katib for lunch. Accepting the money, Katib took hold of the shoeshine box and left Bashir's shop.

"Don't go too far from the city," Bashir warned.

Katib turned, offering a hearty nod, and adjusted the leather strap of the weighty shoeshine box on his small shoulder while softly humming a tune from a Madhuri song.

Bashir watched him disappear in the distance. He shook his head at a thought, then went back to work.

When Katib walked past Rahim's shop, he saw Ali back at work. He was engrossed in teaching another new boy how to wash a car while Rahim barked orders at the other boys. Making sure he wasn't seen, he quickly darted into another alley.

8

The Income Support

"Did your bhabi sign up for the income support program?" a man asked while reading a newspaper as Bashir polished his shoes. Bashir frowned at the question.

"Sahib, I am not interested in charity," he said.

"Oye, it's not charity." The man laughed softly. "It's support from the government for widows. Don't be stupid and get it, or you'll miss a good opportunity."

Bashir contemplated, then asked, "Sahib, what should I do?"

"Take your bhabi to the Nadra office; they have income support for widows," the man said, not taking his eyes off the paper. "They will guide you."

As Bashir contemplated, his hand slowed to a halt, alerting the man. "Oye," the man snapped, throwing a fleeting glance at Bashir, "stop daydreaming and do my other shoe. I have to be somewhere."

"Yes, Sahib." Bashir quickly finished the first shoe and adjusted his brush onto the other. "Thank you for the information, Sahib."

"Okay, okay. Hurry up; I told you I need to be somewhere,"

the man said.

After Bashir finished, the man inquired about the cost of the shoeshine.

"Twenty-five rupees," Bashir informed.

"Twenty-five? That's too much." The man shook his head. "I will only give you ten rupees."

Before Bashir could argue, the man pulled out ten rupees from his wallet, tossed them near Bashir, and left. Bashir picked up the money and placed it in his small money box without raising any objection.

Later that evening, Bashir and Rukhsana rode the Metro to the Nadra office.

It was Rukhsana's first ride on the Metro bus; she never had the chance to travel before. She used her chadar instead of dupatta, covering everything from tiny strands of hair to her ankles. Bashir made no changes to his attire and stuck to his regular shalwar Kameez.

"Tell them you are a widow. We have no money. Convince him that we need income support," Bashir told Rukhsana before boarding the bus.

On the bus, a wall of bodies pressed tightly together greeted him. With no choice but to wedge himself between the clustered men grasping the pole for support, he felt crushed, each breath a struggle in the confined space.

Meanwhile, Rukhsana navigated her way through the sea of women, searching for a space in the front section of the bus designated for them. With effort, she maneuvered into a spot surrounded by chatter and the rustle of colorful fabrics.

The Nadra office mirrored the bus's chaos. Bashir found a spot in the men's line, and Rukhsana stood in the less-crowded women's section beneath a droning ceiling fan.

"Oye, I was standing here; I just went away to get my form," a man said, approaching Bashir and waving a Nadra form.

"I don't care; now I am standing here," Bashir said firmly.

"Are you serious? Everybody knows I was standing here." The man shook his head in exasperation. His eyes darted around, seeking validation from others.

"I am not moving! Leave me alone!" Bashir snapped, his voice sharp and firm.

The man pressed in behind him, muttering under his breath.

Sahib, I am a widow. I have two little children. Please, sign me up for income support. Rukhsana practiced under her breath as the line moved.

"CNIC, please," the receptionist asked Rukhsana as she moved forward for her turn and delivered her lines as rehearsed.

"The what, Sahib?" Rukhsana frowned, rocking Kanji on her hip.

"Your identity card, bibi," the receptionist commanded.

"I don't know about it," Rukhsana uttered uneasily.

"You do not have an identity card?" The receptionist raised his eyebrows.

"Wait, my brother-in-law might know about it," she said, "I'll go and get him."

As the men's line inched forward, tensions began to simmer among the weary crowd.

"You seem uneducated, hence the lack of manners," the man behind Bashir grumbled, loud enough for others to hear. "Everybody knows I was standing here."

Bashir, trying to keep his composure, ignored the comments. However, as the minutes dragged on, the man's impatience grew. He began complaining about Bashir audibly, making heads turn. Bashir turned to confront the man, but before he could, he saw Rukhsana waving at him, urging him to come forward.

Bashir wove through the men's crowd to get to the front, provoking the anger of those waiting in line.

"First, he took my spot, and now he's jumping the queue!" the man behind Bashir shouted.

"You are cutting in line!" another man seethed, but Bashir paid no attention, pushing forward until he reached the receptionist's window.

"He is asking about an identity card," Rukhsana informed, urging Bashir to produce his own identity card.

"Sahib, here's my identity card." He slipped the card toward the receptionist through the circular glass opening in the window.

Meanwhile, the men's voices grew louder, bellowing at Bashir to return to the line and wait his turn. Bashir remained steadfast, paying no heed to their demands.

The receptionist examined Bashir's identity card and asked, "Is she the widow? Where is her identity card?"

"She is a woman. She doesn't need a card." Bashir scoffed.

"Everybody needs an identity card. The line for the identity card is to your left. Now move over," the receptionist said, shaking his head in disbelief.

"She is my bhabi, Sahib. My brother passed away," Bashir insisted.

"The income support is for the wife and the kids, not for brothers. Bring her identity card. I can't process her application without that." The receptionist waved Bashir to move away from the window.

"But Sahib, no woman in our family has the card." Bashir shifted uneasily, his eyes searching the receptionist's face for any sign of understanding or empathy.

"That is not my problem," the receptionist dismissed.

"If I don't have her identity card, I won't receive income support?" Bashir's voice escalated as he barked at the receptionist, slamming his palm against the glass window, a behavior Rukhsana was familiar with. She promptly seized Bashir's arm to calm him down.

"No. As I said, the support is not for you." The receptionist shook his head, adjusted his glasses, and again waved his hand to signal Bashir to move away from the window.

The man from the line reached the front and gave Bashir an aggressive tap on the shoulder.

"Get back to your spot!" the man commanded in a thundering voice.

"Don't touch me!" Bashir exclaimed sharply.

"We have been waiting here for hours!" the man erupted.

Bashir swatted the man's hand away with a swift motion, his expression hardening with defiance. However, the man retaliated by seizing Bashir's collar with a firm grip. In a surge of adrenaline, Bashir reacted and shoved the man forcefully into the crowd, knocking into several others and drawing them into the fight.

"Guards!" The receptionist rose from his seat as punches began to fly.

Rukhsana begged, her voice breaking with sobs, but Bashir couldn't hear anything anymore. While others watched in horror, he launched a relentless torrent of punches into the man's face, pulverizing it.

9

IND vs PAK

10:40 A.M.

Katib struggled to adjust to the leather strap that kept slipping off his small shoulder. He found himself constantly readjusting it to ease the burden, even attempting to switch shoulders, only to find that option just as uncomfortable.

"Shoeshine, only fifteen rupees!" he shouted as he walked through the streets of the Old City. If someone passed too close to him, he raised his voice to ensure they heard the sales message.

After a few hours, Katib had only earned thirty rupees, not good enough to please Bashir. Feeling exhausted, he settled onto the cement stairs of a shop to catch his breath.

"Choka!" echoed a salesman's shout within a nearby shop, prompting the shoeshine boy to turn his head in curiosity.

He pushed his shoeshine box closer to the shop's window and climbed on it to peer inside. A few shopkeepers were huddled around a small TV, their faces lit up with the glow of the screen.

Katib pushed his shoeshine box further to look at the TV screen: a cricket match was on. It was no ordinary match; it was India versus Pakistan in an ODI.

Moments later, Shahid Afridi appeared on the screen, ready to bat against India. Katib watched with a big smile, forgetting about the shoe shining and the money he needed to earn before heading home.

"Oye!" A salesman noticed Katib. "On your way, stop blocking the window." He waved his hand to steer the boy away, forcing him to jump down from the box, carry it hastily, and scamper off.

* * *

11:30 A.M.

As some lazy shopkeepers began their day, yawning and stretching while they opened their shutters, Katib had already strolled through a dozen alleys and visited various shops in search of customers. He had collected forty rupees and a few coins that jingled softly in his pocket with every step.

With his lunch money, he bought a spicy corn on the cob. He placed his shoeshine box beside him on the sidewalk and devoured the yellow tidbits while watching the traffic on the road. As he scarfed down the last row of kernels, he let his eyes wander, observing the bustling traffic on the road. Suddenly, something caught his attention on a nearby mountain of trash: a leather shoe, its worn surface peeking out from the heap of refuse.

Katib hurriedly finished the corn, wiping his hands on his kameez before scrambling up the trash pile for a closer look.

Who would throw out such a good shoe? he wondered as he gingerly extracted it from the rubbish. The leather, though scuffed, still held a certain dignity. He brushed away the debris and eagerly tried it on. It was quite large, twice his size, but that didn't diminish his excitement. Despite its poor fit, he felt an inexplicable urge to keep it.

"I will wear it next Eid," he murmured to himself, picking away more debris from the shoe and pondering the ideal occasion for its use. *By next Eid, my feet will be big enough to fit.* Katib smiled at the thought, but the smile quickly vanished as he realized the problem: its mate was missing.

10

Gul Khan and the Fifty Plastic Bottles

After a few minutes, Katib was back on the trash pile in pursuit of the other shoe. The heap, a mountain of neighborhood junk containing everything from old clothes to baby diapers, shifted and crunched under his feet with every step. The smell of decaying waste filled the air, making him wrinkle his nose in distaste. Determined, he sifted through the garbage, his hands pushing aside moldy cardboard and broken toys as he ascended.

Suddenly, he stopped. Someone else was up there, too.

Gul Khan, a skinny, pale Pathan boy with a garbage bag slung over one shoulder, sifted the garbage with the other leather shoe cradled in his arm. He stopped and regarded the shoeshine boy. He seemed to share the same goal: finding the mate of the leather shoe.

He wore a tattered oversized green T-shirt with stains. His forehead had a small blackish cyst. He was barefoot and without pants, but the shirt covered most of his body. His most prominent features were his rounded shoulders, the lump on his forehead, a locket around his neck, and dirt-filled fingernails visible even from a distance.

What a filthy Pathan, Katib thought. "I found it first," he shouted authoritatively.

"No, I found it first," Gul Khan replied calmly.

"Your feet aren't even big enough to fit in these shoes," Katib argued as he pointed at Gul Khan's dirty feet with soles etched with cracks from endless days spent barefoot.

"Your feet aren't big enough either," Gul Khan retorted, his eyes narrowing with a challenging glint.

Katib stared at him, contemplating for a minute, his brow furrowed in thought. Finally, his face lit up with a sudden idea. "I will give you ten rupees if you give me the shoe," he exclaimed, his voice eager and insistent. He reached into his pocket, fingers brushing against the edges of a crumpled ten-rupee bill, ready to make the exchange.

Gul Khan considered the offer for a second. "I will give you two plastic bottles if you let me have the shoes," he proposed, his voice earnest yet hesitant.

Katib frowned. "What will I do with the plastic bottles?"

"You can build things with bottles." Gul Khan rummaged in his garbage bag and pulled out two bottles, holding them up like a salesman showcasing his wares. Each bottle had colorful straws and bits of twine jammed inside them.

Katib frowned at the bottles. "What is this?" he asked.

"This is something I built," Gul Khan said proudly.

"I don't want them," Katib returned abruptly. "And anyway, I have the polish and the brush to keep them clean. There's no point in keeping them if you can't clean them."

"Where is your shoe polish?" Gul Khan demanded, placing his bottles back in the garbage bag.

"Do you promise to let me keep them if I show you my polishes and the brush?" Katib asked.

Gul Khan considered for a moment, his eyes narrowing in thought. "Okay, show me, and then I will decide," he said finally, his voice firm with resolve.

"Follow me," Katib replied, leading the way with purposeful strides.

He guided Gul Khan to the opposite side of the cluttered heap to show him his shoeshine box and the assortment of polishes he owned. However, upon arrival, to his dismay, it was nowhere to be found.

"It was ... right here. I left it here," Katib stuttered, panic creeping into his voice. He felt both embarrassed and crushed, unable to face the prospect of another failure upon returning home.

Observing Katib's fruitless search for the shoeshine box, Gul Khan pondered whether Katib had fabricated its existence just to acquire the other shoe.

"I swear, I left it right here." Katib pointed at where he had left the box. Gul Khan couldn't care less; he couldn't wait to have the other leather shoe and be on his way.

"Maybe I can have the shoe now?" he said.

"No!" Katib bellowed in agony. "Don't you see? Somebody has stolen my shoeshine box!"

I don't care, Gul Khan thought.

"I have to go. I don't think you have the shoe polish—"

"I have it!" Katib screamed at the Pathan. "You have to believe me!"

Gul Khan scratched his head, "How do I know you are not lying?"

"I am not!" Katib exclaimed.

"Psst," came a sudden whisper.

Katib turned to find a homeless man seated near a pile of discarded belongings. He beckoned Katib urgently by tapping his dirt-filled fingernails lightly on the ground.

Katib hurried toward the homeless man, his heart pounding.

The man sat cross-legged on a flattened piece of cardboard, his ragged clothing barely holding together.

"I think I know who took your box," the homeless man said, his voice a raspy whisper.

"Who?" Katib asked with rising impatience.

"Give me a twenty, and I shall tell you," the homeless man said, stretching his hand toward Katib.

Katib hesitated for a split second, then reached into his hidden shalwar pocket and immediately produced a crumpled twenty-rupee bill. He offered it to the homeless man without skipping a beat, his eyes never leaving the man's face.

The homeless man took the bill, examining it closely to ensure its authenticity. Satisfied, he nodded and tucked the bill into a concealed pocket within his own tattered shalwar.

"A Pathan kid took it," the homeless man said, glancing at Gul Khan. "He had the same bag as him."

Gul Khan's eyes widened in recognition. "Oh, Moosa!" he remarked. "He sometimes collects wooden items, although he is not supposed to."

The homeless man shrugged, his interest waning. "That's all I know," he said dismissively, turning his attention back to his meager belongings, signaling the end of the conversation.

"You know him?" Katib turned to Gul Khan. The Pathan acknowledged with a subtle dip of his chin.

"Will you take me to him?" Katib's voice quivered with mounting anxiety.

Gul Khan's eyes darted to the leather shoe in Katib's hands.

Katib lowered his eyes to the shoe and sighed plaintively.

* * *

12:45 P.M.

Gul Khan cradled both leather shoes in his arms like a Christmas present while barefoot. Katib walked alongside him, his eyes repeatedly drawn to the leather shoes with longing.

"Why don't you wear them?" Katib asked, unable to keep his eyes off the shoes.

"I will wear them when I visit my mother," Gul Khan answered as he spotted a trash pile and started sifting it for plastic bottles.

"Can we go find Moosa now?" Katib asked impatiently.

"No," Gul Khan said, sifting carefully. "I need to collect bottles before someone else takes them."

"But I need to find my shoeshine box now," Katib said as he watched Gul Khan sift the garbage.

"Well, you could help me speed things up." Gul Khan inspected a plastic bottle. "I am not going home without selling bottles."

Katib considered for a moment and then moved in to help despite himself. There was something bigger at stake here: his reputation before Bashir. He couldn't afford to disappoint him again, or he'd work in the shoe repair shop for the rest of his life, the notion he despised the most. So he sifted as fast as he could to help Gul Khan.

Gul Khan was shy and reserved. He kept his gaze to himself or his activity. He spoke with small pauses and carefully chosen words, as if not to make any mistake, unlike Katib, who spoke with confidence. It intimidated Gul Khan a little. Katib could decipher the lack of confidence in Gul Khan, and he liked it. It made him feel superior to the Pathan in some way.

"When can we see Moosa?" Katib inquired as they traversed through heaps of garbage littering every corner.

"I have to collect at least fifty bottles before I go home." Gul Khan inspected a bottle before tossing it back in the garbage.

"How many do you have now?" Katib asked, his impatience rising.

Gul Khan looked over his shoulder toward his bag and replied with a shrug, "I don't know, but they are not fifty."

Katib looked at Gul Khan's bag: the empty interior caused the sides to sag. "How do you know when they are fifty?"

"The bag will be full when there are fifty."

"Why do you have to collect fifty?"

"One garbage bag can fit around fifty bottles, and I need to sell at least one bag."

"What happens if you don't?" Katib pressed.

"Then I'll make less money," Gul Khan said, pausing briefly to glance at Katib before resuming his search. "The more bottles, the more money, and the sooner I can return to my mother."

"Is Moosa your brother?" Katib questioned after a minute of silence.

"No," Gul Khan replied, eyes on the garbage, sheer concentration.

"Then how come you live together?" Katib knitted his brows.

"His mother is poor and lives in a faraway village. So we live with Lala to make money." Gul Khan sauntered toward another garbage pile.

"Where is your mother?" Katib followed him to the other pile.

"She also lives in a faraway village."

"So, you have no siblings?"

"I don't know. Lala has only told me about my mother."

Gul Khan found a few empty Pepsi plastic bottles and placed them in his bag. Katib tried to put a bottle in Gul Khan's bag, but Gul Khan shook his head in disapproval. The bottle had multiple fractures, making it unsuitable for a successful sale.

"Try to find bottles with fewer marks on them," Gul Khan said. "The better the condition of the bottles, the more money the recycler will pay for them."

They crossed the Lahori Gate and walked away from the main road. The bustling sounds of the market began to fade as they ventured further away, replaced by the occasional chirping of birds and the roar of a distant rikshaw. Just a few miles from the main road, they encountered a hookah maker seated cross-legged on a colorful woven mat. He was engrossed in his craft, adding ornamented garments and glimmering tiny round mirrors around the twisting pipe of a hookah. He had two empty Pepsi plastic bottles placed near his mat with faded and crinkled labels. Gul Khan studied them for a moment before approaching the man.

"I need them for water," the hookah maker refused politely without taking his eyes off his craft or cutting short the process; he continued adding the ornamented garment to the hookah skillfully.

"I could really use them," Gul Khan insisted.

The hookah maker glanced at the Pathan before lowering his gaze back to work and murmured, "I need them," forcing the boys to turn away from him.

"There is much more trash near Delhi Gate," Katib offered.

"Are you sure?" Gul Khan scratched his head, furrowing his

brow in doubt.

"I have seen trash there." Katib shrugged.

"You better not waste my time," Gul Khan muttered.

The boys walked alongside the debris-cluttered narrow streets, flanked by decrepit buildings and shops with faded paint and crumbling plaster. Somewhere, empty plastic bags swirled in the air like kites, while empty potato chip wrappers, helpless against the wind, mimicked their movement on the ground. Amidst this silent chaos, the occasional bark of a stray dog or the shout of a street vendor pierced the stillness.

"Is Lala your father?" Katib asked, his eyes keenly scanning the surroundings. Spotting a plastic bottle in the distance, he swiftly darted ahead to retrieve it.

"No," Gul Khan replied, adjusting the bag on his shoulder. "We just live with him. Once we have enough money, we will go to our mothers." His tone was matter-of-fact, indicating a desire to keep the conversation brief. Gul Khan hoped Katib would take the hint, but instead, his succinct response seemed to pique Katib's curiosity even more.

Katib placed a plastic bottle in Gul Khan's bag as they continued. He had learned to pick the bottles worth a sale.

"Does Lala beat you?" Katib asked after a minute or two of silence, his voice hesitant but curious.

"No. Never," Gul Khan replied without hesitation, his hands continuing their careful work.

"Does he scold you?"

"No."

"He sounds like a good guy."

"What about your parents?" Gul Khan asked. He wasn't sure if he should start a conversation with an unknown boy. Lala never encouraged meaningless conversations with strangers.

"Just mind your own business," Lala would say. "Don't waste time."

"My father died a few months ago," Katib replied, wretched at his absence. The thought brought back memories. Katib remembered the day he walked into his house and heard his mother sobbing with her face buried in her hands.

"How did he die?" Gul Khan asked. They adjourned bottle-sifting for a moment.

"I don't know," Katib replied with a shrug. "I live with my mother, sister, and uncle. He's angry all the time,"

"What does your sister do?"

"Nothing, she just sleeps mostly. She can't walk yet, but ma says after a few years, she'll send her to ma'am Zubeda's house for housekeeping work," Katib said as they resumed the sifting process. The junk had a lot of tin cans and plastic bottles, but few would make a good sale.

They walked in silence for a moment, looking for another garbage pile.

"My name is Gul Khan," Gul Khan paused and offered his hand to Katib, who wasn't sure if he should shake his dirty hand with dirt-filled fingernails.

"I am Katib," he said as he shook the Pathan's hand. Afterward, he swiftly wiped his hand on his Kameez as if to rid himself of any potential germs from the contact.

"If you want, you can come to my house. I can make tea for you," Katib offered. "You can also use our soap if you want."

"No, thank you," Gul Khan walked on, scanning the area for plastic bottles. "I had tea with breakfast. Lala always says we shouldn't have it more than once a day, and I've no use for soap right now."

"Do you want to eat choran?" Katib said after a pause.

"What is that?" Gul Khan turned to him.

* * *

Katib ripped open a choran package and emptied the content into Gul Khan's palm. The Pathan licked it off his palm, and the moment it touched the tip of his tongue, his face contorted.

Katib laughed; he was expecting that reaction.

"It is really spicy." Gul Khan licked the rest of the choran off his palm.

"And delicious," Katib added, licking his own palm. They ripped open another bag of choran and licked it off their palms.

11

Lala's Shanty

When he came back, the shanty was empty. He always got home before any of the boys to clean, pray the Zohar prayer on the namaz mat, and prepare hot water for tea on a gas stove.

He was fit despite his advanced years. An eye patch covered his left eye, and a slightly visible limp made him walk slower. A loose, hand-stitched gown, patched up in several places, hung from his body. He wore various amulets around his neck that would swing back and forth because of the limp. A few white strands in a sea of dark hair gleamed whenever he stood under the ceiling light.

The shanty consisted of two primary sections: a spacious area housing a table, a small bookshelf with religious texts, a closet, and a small room with threadbare mats where boys would sleep. A pendant light bulb, hanging low from the ceiling, illuminated a stack of floor cushions directly beneath it, their fabrics faded and torn. An old wooden table in the corner carried a collection of mismatched pots and pans, a well-used tea kettle emitting a faint whistle, and a few worn plastic disposable spoons scattered haphazardly.

He poured hot water into a chipped mug and sipped thoughtfully, his gaze fixed on the cupboard in front of him. After a prolonged moment of contemplation, he set down his drink and approached the cupboard, unlocked it, and retrieved a small steel box. Placing the box on the table, he reached into his shirt's inner pocket and withdrew a collection of crumpled bills and coins. Carefully counting the money, he then secured it with a rubber band before placing it inside the steel box.

He then grabbed a schoolbag, opened it, and pulled out a few wallets, sifting through their contents. Among them, he picked out a wallet, pulled out a couple of bills, and added them to the cash in the steel box. Behind him, the door swung open with a croak announcing someone's arrival. He placed the steel box inside the closet before turning toward the door.

Gul Khan and Katib emerged from behind the door to find him looking at them with a gentle smile that radiated affection and sparked an instant likability.

Gul Khan placed his garbage bag on the floor and threw himself on him for a hug. "As-salāmu ʿalaykum, Lala." He wrapped his arms around him.

"Waʿalaykumu as-salām, my boy." Lala hugged him back affectionately while studying the guest.

"As-salāmu ʿalaykum." Katib approached Lala and offered his hand for a handshake. Lala took his hand and pulled him in for a hug. "Waʿalaykumuas-salām," he replied.

"Who is this young fellow?" he asked Gul Khan.

"He is Katib. He lost his shoeshine box, and I think Moosa took it," Gul Khan explained.

"Oh, is that so?" Lala remarked as he pushed the closet door, forcing it to close. Katib's gaze landed on a few schoolbags in the corner before the closet door snapped shut.

"Moosa should collect plastic bottles, not shoeshine boxes." Lala chuckled, but the boys remained quiet, not knowing whether laughing would be appropriate.

"Well, Moosa has not returned yet," Lala went on. "If he has it, you can have it back." He smiled his warmest smile at Katib, which Katib returned with a shy grin of his own.

"What is that?" Lala asked, pointing his long, thin finger, adorned with several silver rings, toward the shoes.

"I found these in the junk near Lahori Gate," Gul Khan said. "Can I keep them, please?"

Lala considered the request and smiled as he took Gul Khan's head and gently kissed his forehead. "Of course, you can."

"Thank you, Lala." Gul Khan wrapped his arms around him again.

"You are welcome. Now, go pray your Zohar prayer," he said. "And take Katib with you," he added.

Gul Khan acknowledged dutifully with a respectful inclination of his head.

"But I don't know how to pray," Katib remarked.

Lala smiled. "That is okay," he said to Katib and then turned to Gul Khan. "Gul Khan, take Katib to the mosque."

After the boys left, Lala's face changed drastically, his eyebrows curling, meeting in the middle of his forehead. The smile vanished.

* * *

"He seems so nice!" Katib exclaimed as they headed toward the mosque.

"Yes, I know." Gul Khan beamed.

"I saw some schoolbags in the closet," Katib mentioned as they reached the mosque. Around them, devotees entered the mosque, leaving their shoes at the doorstep. "I thought you said you don't go to school."

"No, we don't," Gul Khan said as they reached the mosque gate guarded by a guard with a handheld security scanner.

Katib frowned at his response.

"Gul Khan, is this your friend?" inquired the guard at the gate while scanning individuals entering the mosque.

"Yes." Gul Khan ushered Katib toward the mosque entrance. The guard smiled and let them in without a scan.

"He doesn't check me anymore," Gul Khan whispered to Katib with a laugh. "Once you become a regular, he'll never check you."

"That's great," Katib feigned interest.

"Why does Lala have schoolbags in his closet?" Katib asked again as Gul Khan deposited the garbage bag in the mosque's storage corner.

"I don't know," Gul Khan said and then quickly changed the subject. "Do you think it's safe if I leave them here?" He looked around, pondering a safe place for the leather shoes.

"Yes, sure," Katib replied dismissively. He did not care about the shoes at this point; he couldn't stop thinking about the schoolbags. *Is Gul Khan lying? Did he go to school but didn't want me to know?*

Gul Khan hid the leather shoes under his garbage bag so nobody could see them. They both then performed ablution in the mosque's ablution area.

"But you must know what they are for," Katib remarked again.

"No, I don't," Gul Khan said, dismissing the subject as he washed his arms and elbows three times while Katib followed suit, methodically washing his face, hands, and feet.

While praying, Gul Khan couldn't stop thinking about the leather shoes. *What if somebody took them?* He had picked a spot closer to the door to keep an eye on the shoes.

How come Gul Khan knows nothing about the schoolbags? Katib wondered as he followed Gul Khan and others around him.

If I tilt this way, I can see the shoes better. Gul Khan adjusted his gaze and moved slightly toward the left so his eyes could directly monitor the leather shoes under the garbage bag.

I will ask Lala about the schoolbags, Katib thought. *Pathans always lie.*

12

The Pizza in the Garbage

1:35 P.M.

The main road barely had room for pedestrians as cars, buses, and motorbikes jammed every inch of it. A sole traffic officer abused his whistle repeatedly, blowing it with all his might to manage the traffic.

Gul Khan cradled the leather shoes in his arms. Despite Katib's multiple requests, each more insistent than the last, he refused to put them on.

Katib spotted a plastic bottle from a distance, rushed to grab it, and raised it for Gul Khan's approval. After assessing the bottle's condition, he nodded and allowed Katib to place the bottle in his garbage bag.

"I think we got fifty now. Let's go find Moosa," Katib requested.

"No, we have to find more." Gul Khan placed his hand beneath the bag and weighed, gauging how many more bottles he needed. "It's not full yet," he added and resumed the quest.

Katib followed him quietly, stealing another glance at the

leather shoes.

"Did Lala teach you how to count?" Katib still had so many questions. He had already asked a dozen. *How old are you? Where are your pants? Do you not like wearing pants? Is Lala your uncle?*

"Yes," said Gul Khan. "Lala teaches us everything."

Katib decided to ask Gul Khan something that could interest them both. "Do you play cricket?"

"I don't play any games. Lala says games corrupt our mind and body," Gul Khan declared as he crouched down and began sifting through a garbage pile, his hands moving methodically. The stench was overwhelming, but he seemed unbothered, his focus unwavering. Each discarded item was scrutinized before being tossed aside or set aside with care.

"Then you must not know who Shahid Afridi is?" Katib remarked, taken aback by Gul Khan's lack of knowledge.

"No, I don't know," Gul Khan admitted.

"He is the greatest cricket player ever!" Katib shrieked, making the Pathan stop in his tracks and study him in stunned silence for a moment. He turned to the garbage after realizing the conversation wasn't worth it.

"When I grow up, I'll be a cricketer like Shahid Afridi. Ma will buy me a cricket bat and a ball this Eid, and then I will play all day long until I perfect my skills," Katib explained with a wide grin while he pretended to throw an invisible ball toward an invisible batsman.

Gul Khan sifted in silence as Katib passionately praised Shahid Afridi for over 10 minutes.

After a few minutes, when he exhausted his discussion about his favorite batsman, Katib inquired, "What do you want to become when you grow up?"

"I want to go back to my village, to my mother, and live with her," Gul Khan replied.

"Is that your dream?"

"Yes," Gul Khan said firmly.

"I want to be like Shahid Afridi," Katib reiterated, in case Gul Khan missed it the first time. "I know," Gul Khan acknowledged quickly, hoping to avoid further discussion about the batsman.

They approached a litter-strewn empty plot and encountered heaps of trash, with a few stray dogs resting in the shadows of the trash piles.

Gul Khan took the lead, eagerly diving in to search for plastic bottles.

"Do you know where your mother lives?" Katib asked as he jumped in after and started rummaging through garbage.

"No, but Lala knows," Gul Khan replied, his hands deftly plucking out a few bottles from the scattered heap and carefully placing them into his garbage bag.

"What is that?" Katib asked, pointing at Gul Khan's lump on the forehead.

"I don't know, but Lala says Satan has made a little home in my head."

"He lives in your head?"

"Yes."

"Is he there all the time? Can you feel him?"

"I don't know, but I feel his presence when he causes me a lot of pain sometimes," Gul Khan said.

"Why does he do that?" Katib's forehead creased.

"Lala says he enjoys hurting people and doesn't need a reason." Gul Khan shrugged.

"Why don't you just cut it off?" Katib made a suggestion.

"It will go away on its own," Gul Khan countered. "Lala gives me holy water every day. I am sure it will go away very soon."

"Why don't you go to a doctor?"

"Lala says doctors are useless. You should never waste money on doctors."

"I don't like going to the doctor, but my mother takes me when I get sick," Katib agreed and then asked eagerly, "Can I touch it?"

Gul Khan, with a nod of approval, watched as Katib cautiously reached out to feel its surface.

"Does it hurt when I touch it?"

"No, it hurts when I wake up in the morning and sometimes at night," he said. "It used to be small. I don't know why it keeps getting bigger."

Maybe it's because of the lack of hygiene. Katib thought as he observed Gul Khan's filthy shins, feet, and hands. Even the sides of his mouth had a crusty layer as if a sweet syrup had dried around his lips. *Does he even shower?* Katib wondered and tried to keep his distance from the Pathan in case of lice.

"Look, oye!" Gul Khan shrieked and pointed.

Katib followed the direction of Gul Khan's filthy finger to find a pizza box in the garbage and let out a hearty laugh.

"It's a pizza!" he exclaimed. Within a few seconds, the boys were digging in. Katib found three and a half slices of leftover pizza and two sealed ketchup packets. Gul Khan slurped ketchup from the packets as Katib indulged in a mouthful of pizza. They looked at each other and smiled as if they had accomplished something together.

"They have food!" a child's voice emanated from the other side of the alley. The boys raised their heads to find a group of Jhugi children near the garbage pile.

"Give it to us!" the child demanded, his thin, stick-like finger pointing toward the pizza. Gul Khan and Katib exchanged a glance.

"Why? We found it!" Gul Khan returned.

"This is our plot. We play here every day!" the child exclaimed assertively, his finger still pointing at the pizza.

"So? We play in empty plots, too. Does your father own this plot?" Katib stood up, glaring at the group's leader, who had no intention of putting his finger away.

"You are not going to give it to us?" The leader's eyebrows arched.

"No!" Katib snarled.

"Get them!" the leader ordered, triggering the group to sprint toward the plot.

"Run, Gul Khan!" Katib, with the slices of pizza, dashed toward another alley, followed closely by Gul Khan with the ketchup packets. The children pursued them down the alley in a frenzy of shouts and screams.

Katib and Gul Khan kept running until they lost the children and could no longer hear them.

* * *

Ketchup stained the corners of their mouths as the boys resumed their search for plastic bottles in a garbage pile.

"What else has Lala taught you besides counting?" Katib asked. Gul Khan stopped and studied Katib, deciding whether to trust him.

"Come, let me show you." Gul Khan smiled.

They walked through the heavy midday traffic, shielding their faces from the sun with their hands against their foreheads.

Katib followed Gul Khan as he stopped by a car and pleaded with the man behind the wheel: "Give in the name of Allah, sir. May Allah protect you, sir, please?" The man ignored. Gul Khan immediately moved to another car without wasting time, with Katib right behind him, observing.

"Please, sir, give me some money in the name of Allah. I haven't eaten anything, sir," Gul Khan pleaded with another man. The man in the car grabbed a few coins from his dashboard, handed them to Gul Khan, and quickly brought the window glass up.

Katib followed Gul Khan as he went from one vehicle to another, begging for money. When Katib had seen enough and learned enough, he went to a car and followed the begging procedure, as demonstrated by Gul Khan.

"Sahib, give me in the name of Allah, please. I am hungry," Katib implored. The man, moved by Katib's plea, handed him a ten-rupee bill and rolled up his vehicle's window. Katib gratefully pocketed the money and hurried to catch up with Gul Khan, who was already making his way towards other cars on the road.

* * *

2:40 P.M.

Beads of sweat crowned their foreheads as the boys sat on a shop's cement stairs to count the money they had begged for earlier.

"How did you know how to do that?" Katib asked, feeling his

fist full of coins.

"Lala taught me that," Gul Khan said proudly. He placed his share of money in his shirt's front pocket while Katib pocketed his money in his hidden shalwar pocket.

"Lala doesn't give you money for lunch?" Katib asked.

"No." Gul Khan adjusted his garbage bag on his other shoulder as they got to their feet, ready to find more bottles.

"Do you buy lunch with the money you get from people?"

"No. I give it to Lala," Gul Khan answered, adjusting the garbage bag to balance its weight on his shoulder.

"Then how do you buy lunch?"

"I don't buy. I ask for it. Let me show you." Gul Khan smiled as he took Katib's hand and walked toward one of the houses on the street. Katib let him lead without hesitation.

Gul Khan pounded on the gate with his fist, the sound echoing through the quiet street, while Katib watched in wide-eyed amazement as if awaiting the next trick from a magician.

"What do you want?" a woman asked, peering cautiously from behind the half-opened door.

"Ma'am, give me something to eat in the name of Allah. I haven't eaten all day," Gul Khan pleaded.

"I have nothing. I am sorry," the woman said apologetically.

"Ma'am, please, I haven't eaten all day. Please, for Allah," Gul Khan pleaded again.

The woman paused, hesitating before shutting the door. Katib glanced at Gul Khan, uncertain whether to stay or go, but Gul Khan remained steadfast. After a brief moment, the woman reappeared with two pieces of bread and a roasted meat. She handed the food to Gul Khan, who accepted it gratefully, before she retreated behind her door once more.

"You are awesome!" Katib announced as they enjoyed the

food at the side of the road. It was the most food Katib had had for lunch. Usually, Rukhsana would cook one small roti for him in the morning. During the day, he would only have a piece of bread or corn. Today, he had hit the jackpot with free money and food. *Chacha is so stupid*, Katib thought. *He works in his small shop all day to earn money instead of begging.* He couldn't wait to go to the road and beg for more money.

"This is not stealing, right?" Katib pondered aloud.

"No. Not at all," Gul Khan assured him. "Lala says they owe us. Allah has given them so much; they must give some away."

"And it is not wrong either?" Katib sought clarification as they finished and moved away from the house to resume collecting bottles.

"Not at all," Gul Khan reaffirmed.

If I can learn to beg, I will never have to work. Katib smiled at the thought.

13

Here's How the Cricket Works

3:35 P.M.

Gul Khan and Katib went to the nearest recycling center, where Pathans would sell many recyclable products (plastic bottles being the hottest item).

The recycling plant manager counted the bottles from Gul Khan's bag, inspected their quality, and placed them on an endless stack of plastic bottles at the back of his shop. He then handed Gul Khan a hundred-rupee bill, which Gul Khan stowed in his pocket.

"Do you think Moosa will be home by now?" Katib asked impatiently as Gul Khan slung his empty bottle bag over his shoulder.

"Yes, but he will go to the mosque for prayer," Gul Khan said as they started to walk toward an alley.

"What do you do with the money?" Katib asked.

"I give it to Lala."

"All of it?" Katib frowned.

Gul Khan faltered, "Yes, why?"

Katib shook his head in disbelief. "That's just stupid. What do you like to eat?"

"Rusks, bread, and tea," Gul Khan said.

"No, that is regular food. What do you like to eat apart from it?"

Gul Khan considered. "I like ice cream. It looks good."

"What flavor?"

"I don't know," Gul Khan said timidly.

"What flavor have you tried? Chocolate? Vanilla?" Katib asked.

"I haven't tried any. I have seen people eat it," Gul Khan said.

Katib shook his head once more. "You need to try things," he said.

He took Gul Khan to the nearest ice cream shop, where they got some change for the hundred rupees that Gul Khan had earned earlier.

"You don't have to give it all to him." Katib smiled.

"Are you sure?" Gul Khan raised an eyebrow.

"Yes. I have done it. Everybody does it," Katib affirmed.

Moments later, the boys were licking their ice cream cones.

Lala doesn't have to know, Gul Khan thought as he licked the vanilla and took a bite of the wafer.

Behind Gul Khan, a shop's TV played the one-day cricket match. As soon as Katib noticed the TV, he immediately rushed closer without worrying about the melting ice cream spilling tiny droplets of vanilla all over his Kameez.

"Uncle, what is the score?" he shouted to the shop owner.

"Four out, seven overs to go," the shop owner remarked, sipping his cola drink. Katib suddenly noticed something on the TV screen.

"Gul Khan, look!" he shrieked, pointing excitedly. "That's

69

Shahid Afridi!"

Intrigued, Gul Khan strolled to the shop and peered through the crowd. Sure enough, Shahid Afridi was there, gearing up to bowl.

"Who plays cricket?" he asked, failing to grasp the significance of the moment.

"Anybody can play cricket. Even you and I can. But international cricket is played by professional cricketers only."

"So if we play cricket, will we be on TV, too?"

"No, only professional cricketers are on TV," Katib informed. "So I'll be on TV one day, but not you," he added.

Gul Khan thought for a second. "I would very much like to be on TV."

"I don't think you can be on TV for collecting bottles," Katib said politely. "But if you join my team, you have a shot."

Gul Khan considered the offer. "Do you think my mother will be able to see me when I am on TV?"

"Of course, everybody can see you on TV," Katib assured.

"Okay, I'll join your team," Gul Khan declared.

Katib studied Gul Khan carefully, gauging his commitment. "Great," he replied cautiously. "But you must accept me as the captain," he insisted firmly. "I will always be the captain of my team. Do you agree with that?"

Gul Khan shrugged nonchalantly. "I don't care. I only want to be on TV."

"Good. One more thing, when we are practicing, you can only call me Captain or Captain Katib," Katib said.

"Okay, captain Katib." Gul Khan laughed.

Katib smiled. "I think we'll make a great team. Tell me, what do you know about cricket?" he asked with sheer seriousness as if it were a matter of life and death.

"Nothing," Gul Khan said distractedly, all of his focus on the ice cream.

"Okay, listen very carefully because if you want to be on my team, you need to know how to play," Katib said.

"Can I just sit and watch?" Gul Khan sighed, feeling weary at the mere thought of playing.

"No! You have to participate," Katib exclaimed, incredulous that Gul Khan would pose such a silly question. "You have to be on the field with me."

"Fine, tell me about cricket." The Pathan sighed again.

"There are two teams with eleven players. One does the batting while the other does the bowling. At the moment, India is on the batting, and Pakistan is on the bowling," Katib explained, his eyes glued to the TV screen, paying no mind to the melting ice cream dripping over his hand.

"I don't have eleven players yet, but I'll get them," he added. "With you, I only have to find nine more. Do you have any questions?"

"What is batting?" Gul Khan asked while licking his fingers.

"A bowler throws the ball, and the batsman strikes it hard with his bat. It's called batting," Katib explained as they walked away from the shop.

"If the ball crosses the boundary, it's a four. If it goes soaring in the sky, it's a six. There are usually fifty overs in a one-day match ... " he continued as they disappeared into an alley, licking their cones.

14

Moosa Returns

"Where did you find it?" Lala asked.

"On the street. It has shoe polishes and brushes." Moosa hesitated to meet Lala's gaze.

Lala looked at Moosa for a long time, then spoke firmly, "You know you shouldn't take anything other than the bottles." He looked at the shoeshine box, studying it. "It looks worthless. No one will pay a dime for it," he said sharply. "Never collect worthless junk!"

"Yes, Lala." Moosa acknowledged with a dutiful nod.

"I am sorry," he said as he slowly placed his bottle bag down, his gaze fixed on the ground, not daring to look up at Lala.

Lala took his head in his hands and gently kissed his forehead, "Good boy, now go for your Zohar prayer." He then reached into his inner pocket and produced a small chocolate bar. Moosa's eyes lit up with delight as he eagerly accepted the chocolate, throwing himself into Lala's arms for a tight hug. Lala responded instantly, enveloping Moosa in a strong embrace.

"Don't tell anyone that you found this, okay?" Lala whispered, his voice barely audible.

Moosa's silent nod conveyed his understanding. Licking his candy bar, he quietly left. Once the door closed, Lala turned to the shoeshine box.

* * *

Using his bare hands, Lala dug into the rubble of an empty plot, his fingers clawing through the dirt and debris with a determined urgency. He buried the shoeshine box deep within the mess, pushing it down until it was completely obscured. Then, he carefully covered the site, spreading dirt and small rocks over the area and patting it down to blend seamlessly with the surrounding rubble.

Moosa, who hadn't ventured far, licked his candy while observing Lala conceal Katib's shoeshine box. As Lala turned to go back to the shanty, Moosa quickly disappeared into another alley.

15

Who is Gul Khan's Mother?

4:40 P.M.

Gul Khan and Katib drank tap water, wiped their wet mouths with their sleeves, and made their way toward a quiet alley in pursuit of garbage.

"Have you ever met your mother? Katib asked, watching Gul Khan inspect a small garbage pile.

"No," Gul Khan said, sifting through plastic bags, used baby diapers, and kitchen waste. When he couldn't find much, he motioned Katib to follow him toward another garbage pile.

"Where does your mother live?" Katib asked, trailing behind Gul Khan. They began with a preliminary inspection of the garbage, followed by a comprehensive sift.

"I told you, she lives in a faraway village," Gul Khan replied. "Only Lala knows where it is."

"Do you know what she looks like?" Katib asked, his eyes narrowing with curiosity.

"Of course," Gul Khan said, a smile spreading across his face. He removed the locket hanging around his neck. "Here, let me show you the picture of my mother. But I must warn you: she is beautiful; don't be jealous," he added with a giggle.

Katib rolled his eyes. "My mother is beautiful too."

"Not as much as my mother, I am sure."

Katib leaned in closer as Gul Khan carefully opened the locket, revealing a small, worn photograph. "Lala specially fixed it for me," he said.

The locket unveiled a picture that left Katib stunned—Madhuri Dixit. His eyes lingered on the image, a mix of surprise and confusion on his face. He looked at Gul Khan and then back at the picture. He turned the locket from side to side and looked at the picture again as if a mere shift in direction could alter the person in the image. It was undoubtedly Madhuri.

"Where did you find this?" Katib asked, pointing at the picture, his voice laced with disbelief.

"Lala gave it to me," Gul Khan said.

Katib looked at Gul Khan once more and then studied the picture again.

"Do you like her?" Gul Khan said, his voice tinged with excitement. "I think I have her eyes."

"She is your mother?" Katib asked, shocked and repulsed. *Madhuri is the mother of a dirty Pathan boy?*

"Yes, isn't she pretty?" Gul Khan asked as a broad smile spread across his face.

"I don't think she's your mother, Gul Khan," Katib observed, his eyebrows curling with disbelief.

"Of course, she is. Lala told me himself, and that's why he gave me her picture," Gul Khan stated confidently.

"Maybe he lied to you," Katib said, still shocked by this new nugget of information.

In a split second, Gul Khan snatched the locket from Katib and placed it back around his neck, his eyes blazing with anger. As he stormed off, he yelled, "How dare you! Lala never lies! Don't you ever insult him again!"

Katib stood still, contemplating a way out of this perplexity.

"She's on TV every day," he shouted so the Pathan could hear him in the distance and consider this helpful information an apology. And it seemed to work: Gul Khan stopped in his tracks.

Later, they stood on the small protruding cement ledge of the tea shop, a place familiar to Katib, watching a Madhuri song playing on the wall-mounted TV. It took them two-and-a-half miles to walk to this side of the Old City, near Katib's house, but the journey was worth the trouble.

Gul Khan watched her transfixed. "She's beautiful, isn't she?" he murmured.

"You don't look like her," Katib said, his eyes glued to the TV screen. He hadn't had the chance to listen to a Madhuri song in the past week. He missed it more than he thought he would.

"She is my mother, Katib," Gul Khan said, unable to take his eyes off the TV screen.

Katib studied him for a moment, frowning at the absurdity of it. "She is not your mother!" he snapped. "Look how dirty you are and how clean and nice she is. How could she be your mother?"

Gul Khan turned to him, a little bewildered, not quite believing the sudden outburst. Katib regretted it the minute he said it. Gul Khan, shaking his head in disbelief at Katib's words, jumped off the ledge and went straight into the tea shop.

"Uncle, can you please tell me something? Where does she live?" he asked Mushtaq, the tea shop owner, pointing his finger at the TV.

Mushtaq frowned and looked at the TV screen. "Why do you

ask?"

"She is my mother, but I haven't seen her in a while. I want to know where she lives so I can go see her," Gul Khan replied.

There was a second of complete silence before laughter erupted in the shop. Mushtaq and his customers laughed uproariously.

Gul Khan looked on, taken aback by the reaction. It took him a minute to realize they were laughing at him and then a few more seconds for his face to turn grave with mortification.

"And she is my wife," one customer joked, eliciting more laughs from the other patrons and forcing the mortified Pathan to exit the shop in haste.

Katib leaped off the ledge and hurried after him, his heart pounding. "Gul Khan, I know where she lives!" he shouted.

A customer in the shop called out mockingly to Gul Khan, "When you see her, tell her Sadiq sends his love." The laughter among the other customers grew louder, their jeers echoing in the small space.

Gul Khan's pace quickened, his shoulders tense.

Katib sprinted, trying to catch up. "Gul Khan, wait!" he shouted again, his voice strained from the effort.

"Go away!" Gul Khan's voice trembled, a mix of anger and hurt. He didn't turn around, his grip tightening around the locket as he fled from the shop and the mocking voices behind him.

"I am sorry!" Katib shouted back. "I can tell you where she lives."

Gul Khan stopped, turned, and considered Katib's apology.

"Do you think I am dirty?" he said with a quivering bottom lip, his eyes filling with tears that had yet to dribble down his dirt-stained cheeks. Katib thought for a second, taking a little

longer than he should. "No, I don't. But she doesn't look—"
Before Katib could finish the thought, Gul Khan took off again.

"Katib, she is my mother. Stop telling me she doesn't look
sick or poor," he protested.

"She lives in India!"

"Where's India?" Gul Khan shouted while rushing forward to
nowhere in particular.

"I don't know," Katib cried. "Stop, please. I can tell you more
about India."

Gul Khan looked at Katib, deciding whether to trust him.

Why did they laugh at me? They don't know me. Gul Khan could
no longer hold back the tears; they streamed down his face like
a cascade of rainwater. He immediately wiped the tears away
with his dirty sleeve.

"Are you going to laugh at me?" he asked.

"No," Katib assured.

"Do you promise?"

"Yes, I promise."

"Okay. Please tell me more about India," Gul Khan requested
with a quivering voice.

"My father once told me it's not that far," Katib said as they
sat on the worn stone steps of a shop.

"My grandfather lived in India, and one of my uncles still lives
there. I know that there is a border between India and Pakistan,
and it's not even that far. My Chacha has gone there to watch
the 14th August Parade many times on his friend's motorbike."

"So all I have to do is go to the border and from there go to
India?"

"You can't just cross the border!"

"Why not? I have the shoes now. I can walk long distances,
so it doesn't matter how far it is."

"No, idiot! It's not about the distance. There are soldiers on the border; they won't let you in."

"Why not? Do they own the border?"

"I don't know, but you can't go to the border. You will have to take a train or an airplane."

Gul Khan took in the new information, staring into the distance, trying to process everything that had unfolded in the past hour.

"Can we not sit here?" Katib urgently ushered the Pathan into another alley.

"Why?" Gul Khan asked, allowing Katib to take his hand.

"Everybody knows me here, and my Chacha's shop is just two alleys away."

They both quickly disappeared into another alley. They found a quiet spot behind a stack of old wooden crates, the area shaded and secluded.

"Can I go there by myself?" Gul Khan asked eagerly.

"I don't know. Tickets are expensive."

"How much is a train ticket?" Gul Khan asked with urgency, his brow creased.

"I am not sure," Katib said. "I think it must be at least a thousand rupees."

"How much is a thousand?"

Katib calculated on his fingers and said, "Ten hundred make a thousand."

Gul Khan looked off in the distance and murmured, "It's a lot of hundreds."

"If you don't mind, you don't look like her," Katib said carefully. "If you look at my mother, you'll notice I look very much like her."

"I have her eyes, I think," Gul Khan's voice quivered again.

He struggled to keep the tears from falling.

"You look nothing like her!" Katib said firmly, still appalled by the notion.

"She is my mother! I know she is!" Gul Khan raised his voice. There was more grief in his tone than anger.

"How can you be so sure? You have never even met her," Katib remarked.

"Because Lala said she is!" Gul Khan rose. "I need to collect more bottles, make more money, and go to India. Tell me more about India," he said with a newfound enthusiasm.

"Today, Pakistan is playing against India," Katib stated.

"I hope India wins," Gul Khan said through pursed lips as he adjusted the garbage bag on his shoulder and began to walk away.

"Pakistan is your country, Gul Khan!" A small crease appeared on Katib's forehead.

"My country is where my mother lives, so I will pray for India," Gul Khan turned to Katib and said somewhat bitterly. Their eyes locked.

"Your mother doesn't even care about you. She is rich and beautiful and still won't have you back. She seems like a bad mother," Katib fired back, fuming.

"You don't know that! Stop insulting her!" Gul Khan growled. "Go find your shoeshine box by yourself!" He adjusted his bottle bag on his other shoulder and ran off, leaving Katib to rue his words.

16

The Bully Named Nafees Khan

5:30 P.M.

"Balu Kuriyo, Wandi De Cheez, Lae Jao," a child's voice rever-
berated in the quiet alleys. A young girl cheerfully handed out
taffy and namak paray to the children gathered at her door for
the Wandi.

Katib clutched the two edges of his Kameez, fashioning a
makeshift pouch to secure namak paray, and pushed into the
crowd. No line. No waiting. Every kid fought for the share of
snacks—those who couldn't get to the front left without the
treat.

Gul Khan sat on a shop's stairs, collecting used straws from
its trash can. After he had gathered a dozen straws, he started to
stuff them in one of the plastic bottles he had collected earlier.
Katib watched him bend straws and insert them inside a bottle
as he walked to him with both ends of his Kameez clasped in his
hand, namak paray and taffy in between.

"Look what I got!" he announced with a smile.

The Pathan paid him no mind and stayed focused on the

straws, bending and arranging them to fit into the bottle.

Katib sat near Gul Khan, quietly enjoying the snack. He offered it to Gul Khan, who turned away, murmuring something inaudible. Katib placed a taffy near him anyway. After a moment, Gul Khan quietly plucked it off the ground and consumed it with his face turned away from Katib.

They sat in silence for a moment.

"Why don't you try them on?" Katib glanced at the leather shoes sitting beside Gul Khan.

"Go away," the Pathan said bitterly.

"I am sorry I called you dirty," Katib said. "You are not dirty. You are very nice," he added.

"You mean that?" The Pathan looked up. Katib averted his gaze, hesitant to meet his eyes.

"Yes, you are nicer than the boys in my alley. They never play with me," Katib said.

"Why not?" Gul Khan frowned.

"I think because they have more money than us." Katib shrugged. "I know one of them has a washing machine at home, and I think his father owns a motorbike, too. One is Nadir; he owns two bats and around four balls."

"They must have a lot of money," remarked Gul Khan.

"Yes, they do," Katib replied, then paused to study Gul Khan's face. "Will your mother let you play cricket with me?"

Gul Khan looked up, considering the question. "I think so," he said.

"I hope so," Katib added.

"Do you think she would like me?"

"Yes. I am sure," Katib said.

"I think she'll be a little surprised to see me after so many years," Gul Khan said as he stuffed the bent straws inside one bottle.

"When did you last meet her?" Katib asked, watching Gul Khan intently as he inserted the straws into the bottle.

"I was very young when Lala found me, so I don't remember," Gul Khan said. "Thank God Lala has her picture, or I wouldn't know what she looks like."

Katib observed Gul Khan, thinking, *There is no way she is your mother, you idiot.*

"What if she doesn't recognize me?" Gul Khan fretted, looking off in the distance.

"If she truly is your mother, she will recognize you," Katib comforted the Pathan and placed the leather shoes before him. "Try them on. Let's see if they fit you right."

Gul Khan looked at him, considering: *Should I forgive him?*

"If you want to wear them in front of her, you need to try them on," Katib insisted.

Gul Khan considered, placed the plastic bottle on the ground, and eased his feet into the leather shoes. While they slid in smoothly, their larger size caused Gul Khan to stumble momentarily.

Katib laughed as he watched him struggle to walk. Gul Khan couldn't suppress his own laughter, his steps faltering with each misstep.

"They look great on me." He giggled with excitement.

"Let me try," Katib said, reaching out eagerly.

"No, you may run off with them." Gul Khan shook his head.

"No, I won't."

"I don't know that."

Gul Khan fell, got up, tripped, and rose again, only to encounter another tumble. They both giggled.

"Gul Khan!" a shrill voice called out from the other end,

piercing through the tranquillity of the quiet alley.

Gul Khan turned to see a 17-year-old Pathan walking toward them with his two friends. They were carrying similar garbage bags on their shoulders for the bottle collection, like Gul Khan's, and like him, they were barefoot, dirty, and in ragged clothes.

"Who are they?" Katib asked, observing the approaching boys with curiosity.

Gul Khan tried to run, but the shoes brought him down hard.

"It's Nafees Khan! Run!" Gul Khan screamed, his face pale and voice quaking with fear. Desperately scrambling to rise, he attempted to flee, but the shoes sent him tumbling to the ground once more.

Katib jumped to his feet to assist, but before he could advance, one of the teenage boys seized him by the neck, forcing him to an abrupt stop. At the same time, Nafees Khan lunged at Gul Khan, yanking him by his shirt collar. His strong hand seized the little Pathan's neck, the grip unyielding and merciless.

"Did I not tell you that this is my territory?" he growled into Gul Khan's face. "You can't take bottles from here. But you don't get it when I'm nice, do you?"

"And whose shoes are these, your father's? Did you steal them?"

"Let me go!" Gul Khan wrestled, trying to break free.

"You must have found them in my garbage," Nafees Khan said, slamming him to the ground with a menacing shove. Meanwhile, his two accomplices positioned themselves strategically, forming a barrier around Katib that left no chance of escape.

"Take them off," Nafees Khan ordered.

"No!" Gul Khan's face contorted into a scowl.

Nafees Khan forcefully seized the little Pathan and yanked the shoes off his feet, all the while laughing, with his two friends joining in the laughter.

"It feels like someone made them for me," he slid his feet into the shoes and declared triumphantly. His friends concurred, showering their approval with jubilant cheers.

Gul Khan sprinted frantically, his breath quickening, but Nafees Khan swiftly caught up, grabbing him by the collar.

"Where do you think you're going?" he demanded, his voice cutting through the air with authority.

"Leave him alone, you son of a bitch!" Katib's roar echoed, making Nafees Khan turn in astonishment.

"Oh, have you found yourself a friend, Gul Khan?" Nafees Khan shoved Gul Khan to the ground and, with a malicious grin, advanced menacingly toward Katib.

"You little scum, how dare you!" he said, landing a stinging slap on Katib's cheek, leaving a bruise, before grabbing him and swiftly turning him upside down.

"Now, say something," he snarled, swinging Katib by his ankles back and forth like a pendulum.

Katib screamed while Nafees Khan's friends reveled in laughter.

Gul Khan watched helplessly. "I won't do it again. Please, let him go," he cried.

"That's what you say every time, you pathetic little coward!" Nafees Khan swung the shoeshine boy, his hands around his ankles, paying no heed to his cries.

One of Nafees Khan's friends seized the garbage bag, while another rummaged through Gul Khan's pockets, pocketing the cash.

Nafees Khan tossed Katib on the ground, checked his pockets for cash, and slapped him again for fun. Katib battled hard to keep Nafees Khan from ripping his inner pocket and taking the money, but he was no match for the assailant.

One boy accidentally hit Gul Khan on his forehead, striking him on the sore lump. The force of the blow sent Gul Khan to the ground, flat on his back.

"I better not see you here again," Nafees Khan warned as he and his friends started toward another alley.

Katib gathered all his strength, charged toward Nafees Khan, and punched him in the back with his tiny fist. It only made Nafees Khan laugh. He pushed Katib away and walked on. They left with the leather shoes, the money the boys had begged for, and the garbage bag filled with plastic bottles.

Katib ran back to Gul Khan and sat next to him. The Pathan remained curled up on the ground with his head in his hands. From the nearby shop emanated an explosion of applause, cheers, and exuberant shouts, which could only mean Pakistan was winning against India.

Katib looked around helplessly, tears forming in his eyes. Despite his efforts to hold back, a single tear escaped, tracing a slow path down his cheek.

17

Katib's Plan

Bashir sat in an empty jail cell with his head in his hands. The rage monster he had been at the Nadra office had long gone, leaving the vulnerable Bashir, the mere cobbler—a man with no money or references to get him out.

Following Bashir's arrest by the police, Rukhsana went home alone with Kanji on her hip. Her parents or neighbors could not offer any help.

"Enough is enough. It's about time he learns a lesson about his temper," her father declared firmly before abruptly ending the call.

Rukhsana slowly lowered the phone, her heart sinking as she stood in the stillness of her quiet home.

* * *

6:20 P.M.

"Does it hurt?" Katib gently placed his hand on Gul Khan's

shoulder. Gul Khan could only nod.

"Let's go home and tell Lala," Katib said, still shaken by the event.

"I can't go home without the bottles," Gul Khan said in a trembling, low voice.

"We'll tell him they took it all from us," Katib said.

"Lala doesn't like excuses." Gul Khan struggled to get up. Katib offered his hand, but he refused.

"Can we please find Moosa, at least?" Katib requested carefully, mindful of the delicate nature of the request.

"I can't go home without the bottles. I told you. If you want to go home, then leave!" Gul Khan got to his feet, tapping his forehead, a failed attempt to relieve the pain.

"I can't go home without my shoeshine box," Katib said, following Gul Khan closely behind.

"I don't care about your shoeshine box!" Gul Khan snapped.

"It's late now. I don't think there'd be any bottles left," Katib insisted. "We should tell Lala."

"I'll find some by myself. You can go home if you want to." Gul Khan retorted as he spotted a trash pile and wasted no time walking toward it.

"Who were the other two boys?" Katib followed Gul Khan to the trash pile as he began to sift.

"Rafael and Wahab. They are his friends. They always do that." A tear rolled down Gul Khan's cheek, fell onto his lapel, and disappeared into the fabric. "They won't let me take bottles. Sometimes, if Nafees Khan isn't around, the other two take bottles from me."

"Why didn't you tell Lala?"

"I told you Lala doesn't like excuses," Gul Khan growled. "If I don't sell enough bottles, I will never go home," he murmured.

"He will never let me go home!' A stream of tears escaped his eyes and disappeared into the lapel.

Katib also sifted as he tried to understand what had happened and how to fix it.

"Do you know where Nafees Khan lives?" Katib asked with a sudden burst of energy.

"I am not sure," Gul Khan said dismissively.

"We can take our bottles back!" Katib exclaimed.

"We can't; they are way bigger than us," Gul Khan rejected the idea, keeping himself focused on sifting the trash.

"We don't have to fight them. We will quietly take our stuff when Nafees Khan is out." Katib bounced excitedly. "We can do this!"

"No, that's foolish!" Gul Khan warned. "Did you see how tall Nafees Khan is?"

Gul Khan found a bottle, inspected it thoroughly to ensure it would pass the quality test at the recycling center, and then tucked it under his arm.

"If you don't fight him, he'll never let you go home. You have to do something!" Katib urged. "Stop being such a coward. Let's get our stuff back!"

Gul Khan considered for a moment. "Can you get the shoes back, too?"

Katib's lips parted into a grin.

18

Take Back What We Lost

7:10 P.M.

People were crammed into small shops, watching Pakistan bat against India. Every time a cricketer scored, the crowd screamed their excitement and forgot all about the trials and tribulations of everyday life.

Nafees Khan didn't share the same enthusiasm for the match as the rest of Lahore. While his two friends hung around tea shops with a TV to watch the game, Nafees Khan did not find the match worth his time.

"We will find out who won," he would tell them. "No need to watch the entire game."

He lived in a packed neighborhood with row after row of shanties. During the day, the boys would collect plastic bottles, and later in the day, they would spend time in the storage, dealing with clients who required storage space for rice, wheat, or flour bags. Nafees Khan held the record for selling the most plastic bottles at the recycling center, which allowed him to enjoy special treatment from the recycling plant manager and the others in his community. He gained celebrity status, and (because of that) people ignored his ill temper and the misdemeanors resulting from it.

After they robbed Gul Khan and Katib, they played Ludo on the rusting metal benches outside their shanties. Nafees Khan hated losing, especially to those he considered beneath him. His two friends would always let him win. But if by any chance Nafees Khan lost, they would earn a plethora of obscenities that would force them into a rematch.

Katib and Gul Khan stood behind a three-foot brick wall, a territorial division for the community, watching Nafees Khan toss Ludo tokens and dice to the ground, throwing another tantrum for a rematch.

"Do you know where he lives?" Katib whispered to Gul Khan.

Gul Khan nodded and motioned Katib to follow him. Hunching over to conceal themselves behind the three-foot wall, they walked stealthily. Gul Khan directed Katib toward a shanty at the far end.

"Are you sure?" Katib asked.

Gul Khan scratched his head. "The one with the flour bags," he said with certainty.

The DIY wooden door was full of small and large cavities, helping the boys peek inside the shanty before they pushed it open. Katib stepped in with confidence. Gul Khan followed him in, ghost-white with fear, craning his neck to inspect the surroundings for any danger. The shanty had a single bed with a torn mattress and a small pedestal fan. A broken chair sat alone in one corner with several garbage bags full of plastic bottles on one side and a dozen flour bags on the other.

"Let's take them all," Katib suggested with a giggle as he moved toward one of the bottle bags.

"All of them? Are you sure?" Gul Khan raised his eyebrows.

"They took our stuff. We'll take theirs," Katib exclaimed, his eyes alight with resolve.

"I am not sure about this," Gul Khan said uneasily.

"Are you a man or a chicken?"

"I am not a chicken!"

"Then let's go and get it," Katib ushered him toward the garbage bags, but before they could proceed, the door croaked, forcing the boys to hide behind the dozen flour bags.

Nafees Khan strolled in, sporting the leather shoes with the air of a proud owner. "Count the bags before you store them, okay?" he barked the order from the door before closing it with a thud that rattled the boys to their core. They watched as the ruffian walked to the bed and removed the leather shoes. He came to an abrupt halt, an uneasy feeling settling over him, prompting the boys to tense up and hold their breath.

When nothing seemed out of place, he turned on the small fan and stretched out on the mattress for a nap.

"You said he plays until eight at night." Katib turned to Gul Khan.

"He usually does," Gul Khan murmured. "What do we do now?"

"We wait for him to sleep."

"He will kill us!" Gul Khan mumbled uneasily.

Outside, Rafael was unloading the flour bags from a pickup truck. The truck driver was a man in his mid-40s but looked older than his age—his skin creased with deep wrinkles, and his lips ebony dark due to years of smoking. He took a slow drag on his cigarette, observing Rafael with a keen eye as he unloaded the flour bags from his truck.

Inside, Katib and Gul Khan could hear Nafees Khan snoring.

"Let's get the bags before he wakes up," Katib urged.

"I'm not going. I don't want to be upside down," Gul Khan declined.

"They are your shoes!" Katib argued.

Nafees Khan's paunch shifted up and down with every loud, annoying snore.

"Could you please fetch them for me?" Gul Khan said, his tone earnest as he gently rested his hand on Katib's shoulder.

"No! I don't want to be upside down, either," Katib refused abruptly.

"Please, I am scared of him!"

"Look." Katib sighed. "You get the shoes; I will get all the bottles. I can't carry everything."

Gul Khan opened his mouth to argue, but Katib interrupted: "You are not strong enough to carry this many bottles!"

Outside, the pickup driver stood scrutinizing the bill with furrowed brows. His eyes momentarily shifted from the crumpled receipt toward Rafael with a hint of suspicion.

"Can you calculate again? How can it be over five hundred for six bags?"

Rafael complied and immediately started to punch numbers on a small calculator. The pickup driver shook his head disapprovingly, taking a long drag from his cigarette, the tip glowing brightly in the dim light. He impatiently observed the boy, his irritation growing, as Rafael fumbled with the calculations for the storage price of six bags, taking far too long.

"First, I will get the bags, and then you get the shoes," Katib proposed like a team leader. Gul Khan nodded like an obedient child.

Katib slipped out from behind the flour bags and stealthily crawled to the garbage bags. He carefully lifted one onto his shoulder, moving gently and quietly to avoid making any noise.

Gul Khan watched, on edge, as Katib adjusted the other bags on his shoulders. He carried the bags across and behind the flour bags.

"Go, get them!" Katib urged Gul Khan into action.

Gul Khan glanced at Nafees Khan's motionless body before lowering himself to all fours.

While Gul Khan slowly approached the shoes, Katib noticed a hole in the straw wall behind him. He rammed his fist into the hole to carve an outlet. When the outlet was big enough, he thrust his head through it. From there, he saw the pickup truck and overheard the driver arguing with Rafael. Quickly, he returned inside the shanty and fetched the bottle bags, squeezing them out one at a time.

"Why don't you weigh them properly and calculate again? I'll come back tomorrow," the pickup driver said. "I can't pay more than I have to. Ask Nafees to do the calculation," he concluded, putting on his cap as he unlocked the pickup door and pushed his withered body behind the wheel.

"We can't store your bags unless you pay. I'll get Nafees for you," Rafael offered. The pickup driver considered as he took another drag of his cigarette. "How about you talk to him, get the numbers right, and I'll stop by in an hour. Store the bags until I come back," he said, prompting Rafael to take the bags to the shanty for storage.

While Katib pushed the last bag out of the outlet, he observed the truck driver starting the truck. Meanwhile, Gul Khan approached the leather shoes. With caution, he glanced at Nafees Khan, whose rhythmic snoring synchronized perfectly with the rise and fall of his abdomen as he breathed.

"Gul Khan, hurry back here," Katib whispered. As Gul Khan

retraced his steps toward the flour bags, Rafael swung open the shanty door, catching sight of him. Gul Khan froze. Rafael, too, froze, assessing the scene. A frown marked his face, followed by a sudden, high-pitched howl that roused Nafees Khan from his nap. Katib promptly launched himself out, landing three feet below onto the mud. With haste, Gul Khan crawled back toward the flour bags, slipped the shoes out the opening created by Katib, and then maneuvered his upper body through it. Rafael leaped after Gul Khan while Nafees Khan tried to grasp the unfolding situation.

"What's happening?" he asked, a mix of shock and confusion on his face.

Outside, Katib ran off with the leather shoes and one of the garbage bags, sprinting toward the pickup truck, which still hadn't started.

The driver tried the ignition several times until the vehicle finally roared to life.

"Hurry, Gul Khan!" Katib cried out as he flung the leather shoes and the garbage bag onto the truck bed.

Inside, Rafael clutched Gul Khan's legs tightly, his voice urgent and strained as he struggled to keep hold. "It's Gul Khan! His friend's outside. Follow him!"

"Where's my bat?" Nafees Khan roared, shedding his human form.

Nafees Khan pulled a broken bat from under the bed and darted toward the door.

"He won't let me go," Gul Khan wailed.

"Kick him! Kick him with your feet!" Katib directed from a distance, climbing onto the truck bed.

Gul Khan summoned all the courage and then—whack, whack, whack! He let his feet pound Rafael's face before breaking free and sprinting straight toward the truck. Nafees Khan wasn't far behind, charging toward Gul Khan in a frenzy, muttering obscenities as he closed in on the boy.

Katib stretched out his hand, fingers reaching desperately to grasp Gul Khan and pull him up.

Unaware of the situation in the back, the pickup driver twisted the radio knob until a folk song blared out of the old speakers. The truck slowly moved toward the main road.

Nafees Khan charged toward them, waving his bat. "I will rip you apart, Gul Khan!" he thundered.

"Don't stop, come on," Katib urged, stretching his arm out.

The roar of the engine drowned out their shouts, and the wind whipped against their faces. Gul Khan's fingers reached out desperately, just inches from Katib's, but the speeding vehicle continued to separate them.

Nafees Khan hurled the bat at Gul Khan, the wooden weapon whizzing past him by mere inches as he finally reached for Katib's hand and scrambled onto the truck.

Nafees Khan's other friends came running outside with their fists clenched, but the truck had already climbed onto the main road, accelerating swiftly. Nafees Khan found himself powerless to intervene.

* * *

8: 45 P.M.

Katib and Gul Khan lay on their backs, their bodies pressed against the rough metal bed of the pickup truck. The vehicle

96

rumbled along the deserted road, the faint hum of its engine echoing in the quiet.

Gul Khan held his leather shoes close to his chest as he stared above at the clear sky slowly turning dark.

"Let's eat ice cream again," Gul Khan said.

"What flavor?"

"Vanilla?"

"No, we'll have chocolate," Katib said. "You won't know what you like unless you try."

"Vanilla was pretty good. I liked it."

"Wait till you try chocolate." Katib smiled.

The pickup truck drove away as darkness enveloped the sky.

19

The Fireworks

When he checked the bed of his truck, he found the boys fast asleep.

"Oye!" The driver's voice jolted the boys awake from their nap. A few minutes later, they trudged back home, holding the garbage bag and the leather shoes like trophies.

"What will you do if you can't find your shoeshine box?" Gul Khan asked.

"Then I will stay with you and Lala." Katib sighed.

This information brought Gul Khan to an abrupt halt. "Really? You would stay with us?" he asked, unable to contain his smile. Katib grinned in agreement.

Gul Khan laughed. "We will have so much fun!"

At that moment, fireworks lit up the night sky as if on cue to celebrate Katib's decision to stay. Their eyes darted up, enchanted as the fireworks roared across the sky, the light reflecting on their dirt-streaked faces.

"It's not New Year's, so why fireworks? Is someone getting married?" Katib wondered aloud, scanning the evening sky lit by unexpected bursts of light. Then, it dawned on him. "We won!" he exclaimed. Gul Khan, still trying to grasp the situation, stood puzzled amidst the celebratory chaos. Katib abandoned the garbage bag, breaking into a spontaneous dance around him.

"We won the match, Gul Khan! Can you believe it?" Katib spun around with his hands raised triumphantly.

Gul Khan laughed. He still couldn't understand why the match mattered so much. Above them, fireworks lit up the whole sky, while in the distance, the cheers and whistles of shopkeepers echoed in celebration.

The night was not as exciting for Rukhsana as it was for the rest of the nation. She waited at the door for Katib to come home.

As the police officers at the station enjoyed Pakistan's win against India, Bashir sat on the cell's floor with his arms wrapped around his knees. He brought his chin up to see the police officers dancing near a small TV set and then brought his head back to rest on his knees.

Moosa was walking home after selling his plastic bottles at the recycling center when the fireworks lit the sky. Just like Gul Khan, he was baffled by the celebration.

He knows so much about things. Maybe he can help me. Gul Khan watched Katib dance, caught up in the rhythm, oblivious to his surroundings. *Perhaps we could go to India together.* He smiled at the thought.

20

Bashir Returns

"Sahib, please, release him. He made a mistake," pleaded Zuraes Baba, Rukhsana's 92-year-old neighbor and the esteemed elder of the community. Rukhsana, after her father's refusal, had sought his help to bail out Bashir. He was one of the oldest and most respected tenants of the Old City. People usually never refused a man of his years.

The police officer considered the request for a moment before responding, "You should see the face of the man he attacked. Acid attack victims look better. The man has pressed charges!"

"He lost his brother a few months ago; he lost control over his emotions," Zuraes Baba pleaded with him to reconsider. "Please, show him some kindness, Sahib."

The police officer considered, shaking his head, convincing himself.

"Baba Ji, you must settle it with the man's family," he proposed, and Zuraes Baba affirmed that he would ensure reconciliation. He did everything to secure Bashir's release, driven by Rukhsana's tearful pleas.

"This time, I am letting you go," the police officer warned

Bashir. "If you cause any trouble again, I promise you'll spend the rest of your life behind bars. Do you understand me!"

Bashir lowered his head and nodded, too embarrassed to look up.

* * *

When Bashir returned home, Rukhsana was awake, sitting by the bed where Kanji snoozed sans souci. She answered the door before Bashir even completed his usual knock.

Bashir acknowledged her briefly and walked to the tap on the other side of the house for a quick ablution. He hung his shoulder scarf on a nail in the wall and rolled up his sleeves.

"Bashir," Rukhsana began in a trembling voice.

He turned to her.

"Katib hasn't come home," she said through tears.

Bashir froze momentarily, ripped his shoulder scarf from the nail, wrapped it around his shoulders, and stormed out. Rukhsana wiped the tears from her cheeks as she closed the door behind him.

21

The Stars

9:20 P.M.

When Katib and Gul Khan arrived, the other boys were gathered around Lala, listening intently. Lala sat on his many floor cushions with the children huddled around him, captivated by his words.

Spotting Katib and Gul Khan, Lala motioned for them to join the assembly. Katib took off his sandals before he approached the old floor mat, while Gul Khan proceeded with his dirty feet after depositing the bottle bag and the leather shoes in the corner.

Katib could not wait to ask Lala about his shoeshine box. He looked around at the other children; they paid him no mind.

"Which one is Moosa?" Katib whispered to Gul Khan, adjusting on the mat near the other boys. Gul Khan pointed to Moosa, the youngest boy, sitting near Lala. Katib scrutinized Moosa intently as if staring could reveal the details about his shoeshine box. Moosa noticed Katib's gaze but quickly returned his attention to Lala.

"You look at the pretty things in a shop, and you want to have them," Lala spoke with his eyes closed as if imagining as he went on. "You ask yourselves: Why can't I wear pretty clothes? Why can't I eat good food? There's an answer, my children, there's an answer. You see, there are two worlds: one we live in and the one we'll live in after we depart from this one. The heaven," he said with great emphasis, "and the hell. Heaven is the most beautiful place with everything you ever dreamed of. My children, people who spend this life for a purpose crossover to heaven, and those in pretty clothes, filling up their stomachs with good food, will not. Why?" Lala's voice rose to an electrifying intensity. He waved his arms as if hypnotizing his audience. "Because they are distracted from their purpose." He lowered his voice to a whisper and then suddenly shot it back up. "And what is the purpose?" He looked around at the children and then said firmly, "Obedience: Follow the commands and remain unimpressed by the material things. If anyone asks why don't you wear nice clothes? You say I don't need nice clothes! I don't need good food! I will have better in heaven!" He then paused for a few moments before continuing, "Satan will try to sneak into your minds and tell you differently. And if you listen to him, he'll make a little home inside and never leave."

Katib's eyes lingered on the lump on Gul Khan's forehead, recognizing it as the presence of Satan. Subtly, he reached up to his own forehead, checking for similar protrusions. When he found none, he sighed with relief.

"My children, your home is heaven. My home is heaven, not this earth. Do you want heaven? Or do you want to burn in the fire for eternity?"

"Heaven," the children shouted in unison.

"Yes!" Lala roared with excitement. "You want heaven! So,

when you look at people with pretty clothes or good food, do not feel bad. Why? Because, in heaven, you'll have better." Lala concluded with a wave of his hand.

Afterward, Lala and the boys gathered eagerly around the simple meal—rusks and lentil gravy.

"Did Moosa bring my shoeshine box?" Katib asked Lala during dinner.

Lala licked his fingers as he studied Katib's anxious face. "He found nothing," he said with a comforting smile.

I am never going home. Katib's heart sank. He could imagine anger in Bashir's eyes, his eyebrows curling; he could see his Chacha clenching his fists while Rukhsana's face melted with disappointment.

"Can I stay with you?" Katib asked in a trembling voice, his eyes wet with tears.

Lala gently cradled Katib's head in his hands and pressed a kiss to his forehead. "Allah has brought you to me. This is your home now."

A sigh of relief escaped Katib.

"Katib is going to stay with us," Lala announced. Gul Khan's face lit up.

"Will you accept him as your brother?" Lala asked.

"Ji, Lala," the boys shouted in unison.

"Shabash!" Lala smiled at the boys and hugged Katib tightly.

Gul Khan and Katib shared a glance, smiles never leaving their face. The rest of the boys surrounded Katib, embracing him warmly, their laughter and giggles filling the air. Lala watched momentarily, then cleared his throat, signaling the boys to prepare for bed.

"Come on. I'll show you where we sleep." Gul Khan took Katib's hand and ushered him into the other room. They found a spot on the worn-out mat and settled in.

The room had no windows—only a ruptured tin roof with jagged edges, casting eerie shadows in the moonlight. Through the apertures in the tin, moonbeams filtered like scattered stars, creating a celestial spectacle within the dilapidated shanty.

"My house roof looks exactly like that," Katib whispered to Gul Khan as they gazed at the glistening holes.

"Will you come to India with me?" Gul Khan asked eagerly, his voice brimming with excitement. "I want you to meet my mother," he added.

Katib did not want to get into an argument again. So, he resisted the urge to say anything about Madhuri.

"No, I'll collect some money, buy a new shoeshine box, and then go back home," Katib said.

"But your Chacha will kill you," Gul Khan cautioned, his face fraught with concern.

"Not if I bring a new shoeshine box and money," Katib explained. "How will you find your mother? India is so big."

"Lala knows where she lives," Gul Khan said, contented.

"You are so lucky to have a famous mother. She must be rich," Katib said after a moment.

"I know." Gul Khan smiled. He looked at Katib, who was falling asleep.

"Katib, let me show you something," he whispered and led Katib toward the empty corner of the room where the tin roof was missing. They lay under the roofless part of the room, staring at the dark sky dotted with stars.

"When it rains, we all sleep out with Lala," Gul Khan told Katib as they adjusted. "Rainwater makes all the mats wet. We have to dry them before we can sleep on them again."

"Doesn't it look pretty?" Gul Khan asked after a moment,

looking at the sky.

"Yeah," Katib agreed.

"You know, you can see animals in the stars."

"I have never seen any, and I look at the stars a lot," Gul Khan said.

"Maybe because you don't look closely. Look, there's an elephant," Katib replied, pointing at the night sky, his finger tracing an imaginary outline among the stars.

Gul Khan turned his head to one side, his eyes narrowing as he focused intently on the stars, the corners of his mouth twitching with the effort to discern the shape.

"No, it's a cat," Gul Khan said, moving his head from side to side.

"A cat does not have a trunk; look closely. It's an elephant," Katib said, pointing again.

"I see a tail," Gul Khan said, squinting.

"Do you even know what an elephant looks like?"

"That's a cat, I am sure."

"Nope."

"Shh," a boy hushed from across the room. They stifled their giggles with their hands pressed against their mouths as Katib kept pointing at the sky, whispering animal names until they drifted off into peaceful sleep.

22

The Schoolbag

10:15 P.M.

Bashir looked everywhere and asked everyone he knew, but nobody had seen Katib.

"I think I saw him near the recycling center," one shopkeeper reckoned. Others just shook their heads.

"Sahib, he has been gone all day," Bashir pleaded with the same police officer who had pardoned him earlier because of Zuraes Baba.

"We can't do anything unless it's over 24 hours. Just wait for a few more hours, and then we'll file a report," the police officer said, his attention absorbed by the paperwork scattered across his tiny desk.

"But Sahib—"

"Wait for 24 hours and then come back. Maybe he'll return," the officer interrupted, his tone firm yet indifferent.

Bashir left the station quietly.

* * *

The warmth of a sunbeam gently caressed Katib's cheek, waking him up. The other boys had already left; the room was empty. Katib could hear whispers. At first, he was reluctant to get up, wanting to sleep a little more. But then he remembered that he was no longer in his home. The thought scared him.

Outside, Lala uttered prayers in a hushed tone with his hand gently placed on Gul Khan's forehead.

Katib emerged from the room and silently took a seat next to Lala. He watched intently as Lala's lips moved in silent prayer before gently blowing on Gul Khan's forehead.

"When will it go away?" Gul Khan asked.

"Soon, inshallah," Lala replied, gently blowing on the little Pathan's head again.

All the children followed a predefined schedule. They woke up around 5:30 A.M., performed ablution, prayed Fajr, and ate breakfast, usually rusks and tea. They would leave at 6:45 A.M. to collect bottles and beg for money. Today, however, Gul Khan and Katib stayed behind as the other kids left for their quotidian work.

"Feeling hungry?" Lala inquired, a smile gracing his face. Katib responded with a shy nod.

Gul Khan sat cross-legged on the mat next to Katib, eagerly awaiting breakfast.

Lala poured steaming tea into paper cups with steady hands, unfazed by the wisps of rising steam. Afterward, with meticulous care, he licked his fingers clean of spilled droplets and selected two rusks from a crinkling plastic bag.

Gul Khan and Katib spoke in hushed voices as they watched Lala arrange the rusks near the tea cups. Their whispers abruptly ceased as Lala placed the tray before them, their hands eagerly reaching out for the rusks.

As Katib ate his rusks with tea, Lala opened the cupboard and produced one of the schoolbags that Katib had seen before. He placed the bag near Gul Khan and gently whispered, "Take Katib with you and show him what to do."

Are we going to school? Katib thought as he finished eating. *But I don't even have any uniform or lunch box,* he fretted.

Without further queries or directives, the boys departed. Katib followed Gul Khan quietly out of the shanty, suppressing the urge to ask questions. This time, Katib also brought along a garbage bag to collect bottles, while Gul Khan wore the leather shoes.

"How long do you think I should wear them?" Gul Khan asked.

"Until your feet get used to them," Katib said.

"I don't want them to get dirty," Gul Khan murmured.

Katib threw a glance at the schoolbag. It was an old bag with faint ink stains; its once vibrant colors faded and dull. On the front pocket, the cheerful face of Dora the Explorer beamed with excitement, her trusty map in hand.

I could put a cricket kit in it, Katib thought. "Why are we taking the schoolbag to the mosque?" he asked.

"I will show you," Gul Khan said with a smile.

"You said you didn't know what the schoolbags were for!"

"I was not supposed to tell you then," Gul Khan said with a pang of guilt.

In the mosque, the boys performed ablution and sat behind a group of men preparing for prayer.

Gul Khan placed the schoolbag before him and whispered to

109

Katib, "We are not going to pray. We will only pretend."

"Why?"

"I will show you. If you want to stay with us, you must learn to do this."

"Every day?" Katib asked.

"No, only when Lala asks."

As the prayer commenced, the boys feigned their devotion. Katib observed Gul Khan as he leaned forward, skillfully delving into a man's Kameez pocket to extract a wallet and discreetly stow it inside the school bag.

Gul Khan then ushered Katib to move slightly to his left, positioning himself directly behind another man, deftly pocketing a wallet, a watch, and a few rupee bills.

"Only stand behind men who are wearing shalwar and Kameez. It's hard to get a wallet out of a jeans pocket. It's not impossible; I have done it. But I don't recommend it," he cautioned Katib as they moved more to the left, positioning Gul Khan behind another man.

"What if we get caught?" Katib whispered nervously, glancing around with wide eyes.

"I have never been caught. But you have to be careful. That's why no jeans," Gul Khan elaborated. "If it's hard to get anything out, leave it and move on. If you try harder, it can alert people."

Gul Khan stole over six wallets, two watches, some rings, and a few thousand rupee bills.

As the boys silently slipped away from the prayer mat and toward the door, Gul Khan whispered, "We can gather much more during Ramadan when prayers are longer. Find things worth a lot of money, like watches and jewelry. You remember the boy with long hair?" he asked. "The one who was sitting next to Moosa?"

Katib nodded.

"His name is Farhan," Gul Khan said. "He once brought home seventeen wallets and three expensive watches. I am trying to beat his record."

"What else can we hide in the bag?" Katib asked as they left the mosque without ringing any alarms. Katib glanced around, ensuring no one trailed them. Gul Khan had done it long enough to remain unfazed.

"Anything, as long as it can bring good value. This one time, I found some fake rings that were actual Gold." Gul Khan let out a gleeful laugh. "Lala was so happy with me that he gave me extra rusks for breakfast."

"This is not stealing, right?" Katib asked, perplexed.

"Not at all. These people have too much and need to give some away," Gul Khan said. "It is only stealing when we take things from the poor. Most people have the wrong concept of stealing; they believe anything you take without permission is wrong. But that's not true."

"Why didn't my parents explain these things to me? I could have made a lot of money." Katib shook his head in disappointment. "If my Chacha had the right knowledge, he wouldn't be a cobbler."

"Because not everyone has the knowledge that Lala has," Gul Khan said. "He knows a lot."

"I will make a lot of money with Lala." Katib smiled at the possibility.

"You will." Gul Khan smiled back.

"What if we kept some wallets?" Katib asked.

"What do you mean?" Gul Khan frowned.

"Let's keep some wallets and hide them from Lala?" Katib proposed, forcing Gul Khan to halt.

"Are you saying that we lie to Lala?" Gul Khan's eyebrows curled drastically.

"Just like the ice cream, he doesn't have to know how many wallets we have," Katib remarked.

Gul Khan studied Katib as if he couldn't recognize him and said, "Katib, I cannot lie to Lala, again. It's wrong."

"Come on, Gul Khan. Just think about all the things we can buy."

"No!" Gul Khan snapped. "We are not supposed to!"

"You are such a coward! Who will tell Lala we took some wallets?" Katib fumed. Gul Khan shook his head in disbelief, then hurried away.

"Where are you going?" Katib stood between Gul Khan and the alley leading to Lala's shanty.

"I am telling Lala. You are not thinking right!" He pushed Katib out of his way and ran off. Katib sighed, watching him disappear around the corner.

"Gul Khan, please stop!" Katib ran after him.

When Gul Khan turned the corner, his heart missed a beat.

Nafees Khan and his two friends, Rafael and Wahab, stood at the end of the alley as if waiting for him. Nafees Khan had the broken bat in his hand, which he had thrown at the pickup truck earlier. He looked at Gul Khan, and a wicked smile unfolded on his face. Without losing a second, the boys seized Gul Khan and dragged him to Nafees Khan.

"Did you honestly believe I couldn't track you down?" Nafees Khan growled, his fingers digging into Gul Khan's neck as he whispered with menace into his ear. "You have crossed the line, boy!"

Katib watched the situation unfolding from a safe distance. Surveying his surroundings, he spotted a broken tree branch lying on the ground. Without hesitation, he seized it, feeling the rough bark under his fingers, and held it tightly, preparing himself for whatever might come next.

"Leave me alone!" Gul Khan's voice trembled.

"What's this?" Nafees Khan grabbed the schoolbag and gave it a gentle shake to investigate. When it didn't produce enough sound to reveal its contents, he started to open it, but before he could ...

"Leave him alone!" Katib barked from the other end of the alley, ready with the tree branch in his hand.

Nafees Khan looked at Katib and shook his head.

"I smell shit on you," he announced, eliciting laughter from his two friends. "It's time to go to the sewer where you belong. Filthy rodent!"

Like a warrior on the battlefield, Katib charged at Nafees Khan, striking his knee forcefully with the sharp end of the branch and continuing his relentless assault. With one hand viciously clawing at Nafees Khan's arm, he struck at his face, arms, abdomen, and anything in his path.

Gul Khan watched from a distance, cheering Katib on: "Hit him! Hit him!"

Rafael and Wahab laughed, watching Katib's petite frame struggle with Nafees Khan's sturdy build.

Nafees Khan did not need their help to fight off a 7-year-old. After several failed attempts, he finally got hold of the tree branch, tossed it aside, and then sucker-punched Katib, sending him to the ground. It all happened in a matter of seconds.

Gul Khan froze in shock as he witnessed Katib's fall. Rafael and Wahab, equally stunned, had never witnessed Nafees Khan strike someone of Katib's age with such force. Their laughter came to a sudden halt as they stood petrified, dreading that if they moved, they too could become targets of that same rage.

"Never mess with me, rodent!" Nafees Khan thundered, his nostrils flaring, skin turning vermilion with anger.

Tiny drops of blood trickled down Katib's nose and onto his chin. Stunned, Katib wiped them with his sleeve as a tear dribbled down his cheek.

"Throw him in the sewer," Nafees Khan ordered while rubbing his arm where Katib's fingernails had left visible marks. His friends complied immediately—they grabbed Katib's lapel and dragged him away. Katib, still stunned, watched as Nafees Khan slowly became a dot in the distance.

Once they were gone, Nafees Khan turned to Gul Khan, who stood paralyzed.

"I just want to be friends with you," he said and suddenly lunged at Gul Khan, forcing him to break into a run. The ruffian's athletic build allowed him to quickly grab the little Pathan by his neck and drag him toward a dark corner of a quiet alley.

"Don't take bottles from my area. Why is that so hard for you to unde—"

Before he could finish, a ball of saliva landed on his face, forcing him to close his eyes. He froze for a moment, then wiped it with his hand and opened his eyes to look at Gul Khan, who looked back with a deep frown and a strange new fierceness he had never seen before. It startled Nafees Khan for a second.

"Leave me alone, or I will punch you!" Gul Khan said through clenched teeth.

Nafees Khan laughed maniacally for a few seconds before becoming gravely serious.

"Go ahead." He brought his face forward, closer to Gul Khan. "Punch me."

Gul Khan locked eyes with him, his breaths labored.

"Go ahead. What's stopping you? Punch me as hard as you can," he challenged.

Gul Khan remained still.

"I said punch me, coward!" Nafees Khan's voice thundered, rattling the boy to the core and causing a visible tremor in his legs. A tear traced a path down his cheek, glistening in the soft light of the distant street lamp. He balled his fist, but before he could raise it, Nafees Khan intercepted; he caught his fist and twisted his arm until the little Pathan started to cry. He then raised his fist and launched it at Gul Khan's face, sending him to the ground.

"Coward!" *Whack! Whack!* He delivered blow after blow to the boy's face, eliciting an ear-piercing shriek from him that drew someone toward the quiet alley.

"Who is there?" someone called out, rushing toward the alley.

Nafees Khan tried to press his palm against Gul Khan's mouth, but the boy dug his teeth deep into his hand, biting hard on the flesh.

As Nafees Khan cradled his throbbing, bitten hand, Gul Khan attempted to flee. However, Nafees Khan quickly ensnared him, locking his elbow around his neck, stifling any chance of escape. Gul Khan's agonizing screams shattered the silence, alerting whoever was nearing. The approaching footsteps hastened.

"What's going on?" a voice rang out, sharp and concerned.

Whack! Nafees Khan slapped Gul Khan hard on his head and then dropped him to the ground for more blows.

"You'll never mess with me again!" Nafees Khan roared, unleashing a barrage of punches at Gul Khan, his fists finding their mark with unrelenting fury. As soon as the little Pathan froze in place, Nafees Khan hastily grabbed the schoolbag and the leather shoes before making a swift departure. A mullah was just around the corner, hurrying to investigate the commotion. He watched, suspicious, as Nafees Khan scuttled away from the alley.

The mullah hurried toward the dark corner and gasped at the sight.

* * *

Nafees Khan reached a quiet alley where Rafael and Wahab waited to join him. Before the boys could run away, Nafees Khan noticed the mullah emerging from another alley.

"He has been following me." He turned to his friends.

"We can't go home. Let's go to the mosque," he ordered the boys, and they hurried away before the mullah could confront them.

They concealed guilt and tension with forced calmness as they approached the mosque.

"What is that?" The security guard pointed at the schoolbag as he flipped the switch on his security scanner.

"It's my younger brother's bag," Nafees Khan said, his forced smile failing to conceal the tension in his voice.

The guard signaled for Nafees Khan to lift his arms. Once he obeyed, the metal detector swept over his body. No Beep.

The same procedure ensued for his two friends, yielding identical outcomes. The guard then grabbed Gul Khan's schoolbag to check. Nafees Khan hoped that he had looked in the bag. But he wasn't too worried. *What could be in there? Probably some straws or more plastic bottles.*

Beep ... beep ... beep ... beep. The metal detector chimed in a steady rhythm as soon as it touched the schoolbag, alerting the guards. One of the guards pulled the zip apart, splitting the bag in half to find the many wallets, a few wristwatches, and an assortment of jewelry. He immediately grabbed his baton and launched it at quivering Nafees Khan. "So you are the thief who's been stealing from the mosque!"

"No! No! It's not mine, it's not mine," Nafees Khan stuttered, staring at the wallets in shock.

The guard seized him by the collar. "I thought you said it was your younger brother's?" he barked, striking Nafees Khan with the baton.

"It's not mine, it's not mine. I lied!" Nafees Khan confessed, but the guard was unconvinced and offered no sympathy or consideration. He grappled with fear and helplessness, emotions unfamiliar to him. Two other guards rushed forward and seized him, folding his arms behind his back. His friends stood frozen, not knowing whether to run off or stay put. The other guards pulled out their sticks and whipped the boys while they ushered them away from the mosque and toward the police station.

"I swear to Allah, I lied. It's not mine," Nafees Khan pleaded. He was more shocked and humiliated than hurt by the constant whipping.

Another guard grabbed the leather shoes, examined them, and placed them near the gate with many other shoes.

The next day, the leather shoes were gone.

23

The Chase

The air, thick with the stench of decay, gave Katib a runny nose and red eyes, while the ominous sewer tunnel stretching into obscurity and the echoes of distant water drips evoked fear. Coated in filth, he fought his way out of the 6-foot-deep sewer. The surface was slippery, making each step a precarious dance.

Nafees Khan's friends had thrown him into the neglected part of the sewer, a place shunned even by sewage workers for the stench that could filter through the hardiest of masks.

I am going to tell Lala. He will beat Nafees Khan up and throw him in the sewer. Katib sobbed with his sleeve against his mouth, cursing the ruffian.

"Gul Khan!" Katib called out as he reached the quiet alley near Lala's shanty, wiping his face with his hands to remove the sewer waste.

Everything seemed eerily quiet. Nafees Khan could still be out there, waiting to throw him in the sewer again. The thought made Katib run toward the shanty, hoping to find Lala quickly.

Katib pushed open the shanty door and found nothing but tranquility.

"Gul Khan!" He cried again. No one was there.

Surveying the vacant shanty in search of answers, he found none. Instead, the silence deepened his fear. Tears streamed down his face until exhaustion led him to sleep on the worn-out mat.

* * *

The audible rumble of his stomach woke him up a few hours later, forcing him to get up and go through the tea kettle and the rusk bags. There was no tea or rusks. He surveyed the place, and his eyes landed on the cupboard. It beckoned him. Katib considered and approached it with deliberate steps.

When he reached the cupboard, he stood before it, hesitating, his hand hovering near the handle. He considered it for a few more seconds, his eyes scanning its surface, before finally deciding to open it. Inside, on the top shelf, a few wallets lay scattered alongside the steel box. Below them, nestled on the bottom shelf, were two worn schoolbags, their zippers slightly ajar.

He checked the wallets, flipping through them with a disappointed frown when they proved useless. With a determined exhale, he then turned his attention to the steel box. Its surface was cool to the touch, a small lock securing its contents. Katib glanced around, searching for the key in vain. Suddenly, his gaze fell upon the safety pin adorning his collar, its metal glinting in the dim light. A plan formed in his mind.

He forced the safety pin's point into the keyhole, maneuvering it with determination until he heard the satisfying click of the lock releasing. As the lid of the steel box opened, Katib's eyes widened with surprise and delight while a triumphant smile played on his lips.

In a flurry of movement, he hurriedly stuffed handfuls of candy and bundles of money into the pockets of his shalwar, the excitement of his find overriding any sense of caution.

"What are you doing?" Lala's voice cut through the air like a blade, freezing Katib in his tracks. A surge of fear shot through him, momentarily paralyzing his movements. Though Lala had mastered a tone of amiability, Katib sensed the underlying seriousness of the situation.

Slowly, Katib turned towards Lala, the steel box still clutched tightly in his hand.

"I asked you a question," Lala repeated firmly.

"Put the box down!" This time, a tinge of anger laced his voice. The usual amiability retired, leaving a belligerent tone that sent a shiver down Katib's spine.

"I said put the box down!" Lala repeated firmly.

Katib looked at the door. Lala, too, looked at the door.

"Katib, don't you dare!" he threatened, lunging toward him in a last-ditch effort to halt his escape. Ignoring the warning, Katib bolted from the shanty, clutching the steel box tightly, urgency propelling him forward.

As Katib sprinted away, Lala reacted swiftly, his determination overcoming the inconvenience of his limping leg. Despite the occasional jolt of pain, he pushed himself forward with his healthier leg, closing the distance between them with each determined stride.

"Katib, stop!" Lala roared.

Katib kept going without looking back, without wanting to

know how far Lala was behind him. Lala charged with all his might, forcing his deformed leg to perform more than its capacity.

"Katib, stop this instant," he barked as he finally grabbed the boy by the lapel, bringing him to an immediate halt. The force of Lala's grip ripped off the loose buttons of Khatib's Kameez, inflicting a massive, irreparable tear in the garment. Lala immediately snatched the steel box from Katib's hand and dragged him back toward the shanty. The commotion drew the attention of the nearby shopkeepers, who looked on, curious.

"Nothing to see here, folks. Go about your business," Lala addressed the onlookers as he dragged Katib brutally by his torn lapel. The observers gazed briefly before returning to their activities. Katib moaned in pain, his hands struggling to free his lapel from Lala's grip. Suddenly, Katib's lapel tore all the way, giving him clearance to slip out and earn a chance to escape. Lala was left with a small, torn garment. He quickly resumed, following Katib. But before he could seize the boy again, a poultry truck collided with him, tossing his body a few feet away while spilling the contents of the steel box all over the street. The screeching tires, shattering glass, and the frenzied chorus of distressed chickens echoed in Katib's ears as he bolted into another alley, the cacophony of the accident fading behind him.

He did not look back; he raced through a dark alley, his heart drumming a frantic rhythm. He kept running until a thought about Gul Khan compelled him to halt.

He found himself torn. He couldn't leave him behind, yet returning wasn't an option either. Lala could be anywhere, waiting for him.

In the quiet alley, he stood in the corner, calculating, his heart pounding like a drumbeat.

* * *

Rukhsana held Kanji close, wrapping her in the warmth of her embrace as she kept her gaze fixed on the door.

Katib's knock was unmistakable—a rhythmic triplet of fist thumps, each thud carrying a sense of urgency. Bashir's approach was equally distinctive—a measured sequence of three to four knuckle taps against the door.

It was past midnight, and Rukhsana yearned for either of the two.

24

They Are Taking Away Gul Khan

Near Lala's shanty, Katib discovered a police van, its emergency lights in red and blue gently flickering. Off to the side, an ambulance stood with its doors open next to an Edhi van. Katib saw a mullah indistinctly chatting with the police officers in the near distance. Two Edhi workers were busy covering a body. They zipped the body bag and placed it into the Edhi van.

Katib hurried toward the shanty without a worry. He knew with all these people around, Lala could not hurt him.

Moosa and the other boys stood by the shanty, watching the Edhi workers place Gul Khan's body inside the van.

"They are taking away Gul Khan," a boy said.

"Where are they taking him?" Moosa asked Katib, who had joined the other boys.

"I don't know," Katib said, watching the Edhi workers.

Moosa and the other boys covered their noses to block the stench from Katib's clothes.

"I have to ask you something." Katib turned to Moosa. "Did you come across a wooden shoeshine box today? It has a leather strap."

Moosa hesitated, meeting Katib's gaze briefly before casting his eyes downward in contemplation. Katib reached into his pocket and extracted a chocolate bar he had stolen earlier, the wrapper crinkling softly. He held it out to Moosa.

"Please, think hard. I really need it," Katib said, hoping his offering would work.

Moosa considered for a few more moments before accepting the chocolate and guiding Katib toward the empty plot.

Together, they sifted through layers of debris until Moosa unearthed the strap of the shoeshine box, wrenching it triumphantly from the refuse.

Katib's laughter of relief was contagious, drawing Moosa into it.

The other boys looked on, wondering why Katib and Moosa were laughing. They soon were occupied by one of the Edhi social workers and a police officer who began to question them.

"Where is Lala?" One boy rubbed his forehead fretfully. "He is always home at this hour."

"Only he knows where my mother lives," remarked another. "If Lala doesn't come back, who will take me to my mother?"

"Yes, only Lala knows where my mother lives," added another boy.

"We don't know, but we'll find him," one social worker assured. The Edhi workers exchanged a glance, perplexed, as they ushered the boys into the Edhi van.

* * *

The flashing red and blue emergency lights cast their glow on his face, revealing a thin trail of blood that had streamed down from his forehead to the cheek. He wiped it off, leaving a visible smear on the skin. Even though the hair obscured his vision, he didn't care enough to stash them behind his ears.

He could see Katib and Moosa. He watched when they placed Gul Khan's motionless body in the bag and took him away.

Clutching the steel box's handle tightly, Lala wiped away another line of blood trickling down from his forehead to his cheek.

He looked on, contemplating for a moment before slipping away into the depths of a dark alley.

25

Katib Returns

I hope he's not home, Katib thought. He looked at the house and wondered if Kanji was asleep, playing, or just sitting on the bare brick floor, digging her fingers into the small gaps between the bricks.

The Edhi worker knocked on the ruptured tin door and waited. With every knock, Katib's heart sank a little.

When the door opened, Bashir emerged, disheveled; he hadn't slept. He looked at Katib, and his face lit up, contrary to what Katib was expecting. Bashir fell to his knees and hugged the boy tightly.

"Oh, Rukhsana," Bashir cried with relief. "Katib's home."

He asked no questions—Where did you go? Did you make a hundred rupees? Why not?—instead, Bashir wrapped Katib in a warm embrace that the boy never expected from his uncle.

"Go inside." Bashir gently caressed Katib's forehead and ushered him in through the tin door. *Was he kind to him only in front of the Edhi worker?* Katib wondered.

He dashed inside, letting his shoeshine box crash to the floor with a clatter. In the room, he found his mother asleep on the Charpai with Kanji.

Katib slipped under the worn Chintz blanket, riddled with holes and loose threads, nestling close to his mother. As he snuggled against her, he wondered about the other boys and Moosa.

Maybe they will take them to their mothers, he thought, drifting off into a peaceful sleep. The tiredness of a long day slowly melted away as if nothing had happened.

26

Katib's Cricket Kit

When Katib woke up, he found himself alone in bed. The room was quiet except for the gentle gurgling sounds coming from Kanji, whose finger was firmly lodged in her mouth. The air was filled with the aroma of boiling tea, teasing Katib's nostrils and stirring his appetite for breakfast.

Quickly getting out of bed, Katib hurried outside. There, he found Rukhsana seated behind the stove, preparing breakfast. With a rush of excitement, Katib ran straight to his mother.

"Did you notice me beside you last night?" he asked, wrapping his arms around her.

"Yes, I did." She smiled as she embraced him, unwilling to let go.

Katib suddenly noticed Bashir looking at him as he dipped his bread in hot tea and brought it to his mouth. Katib avoided meeting his gaze, silently praying to avoid any conversations about his past failures.

"Sit down and eat." Rukhsana poured hot tea into a mug, added pieces of bread, and slid it toward Katib. As Katib sat down to eat, he noticed a plastic bag near the door. It was a new shopping bag that could only come with newly purchased items.

"What's that?" Katib asked, slowly chewing his moistened bread, his eyes never leaving the shopping bag. Rukhsana giggled, and Bashir couldn't help but smile, probably for the first time in a long time.

"Do you want to take a look?" Rukhsana beamed. Katib interpreted her smile as an invitation to explore the bag. He rushed toward it, untied the knot, retrieved a package, and tore it open to reveal a cricket kit featuring a bat designed for children under twelve, a green ball with 'Jeevae Pakistan' visibly engraved, a pair of gloves, and a helmet.

Katib could barely contain his excitement as he flung the ball in the air and sprinted to catch it on the other end.

"Wait," Bashir interjected, forcing the boy to release the ball.

"Come here," he called, gesturing. Katib hesitated for a moment before proceeding toward his uncle.

"I purchased that kit for three hundred rupees." He grabbed Katib's wrists.

Katib stood still, concern creasing his brow.

"Do you have three hundred rupees?" Bashir asked. Katib shook his head, avoiding eye contact with his uncle by shifting his gaze to the wall behind him.

"How did you feel when Rahim beat you?" Bashir asked, tightening his grip around the boy's wrists.

"Scared," Katib said.

"Do you ever want to feel that way again?"

"No, Chacha." Katib looked at Bashir, avoiding his eyes, then adjusted his gaze back to the wall.

"Then never try to steal again." Bashir let the boy's wrists slip out of his hands.

"What if I beg for money and food?" Katib asked.

"What?" Bashir stared at Katib in disbelief, then threw a glance at Rukhsana as if it was her fault. Rukhsana's face lost all color.

"I mean, if people willingly give me their money—"

"No!" Bashir snarled. "You only earn it!"

"Bashir, I'll talk to him." Rukhsana intervened quickly. Bashir took a deep breath and then went back to his breakfast.

"Now," he began again, catching Katib's attention just as he was about to return to the bat and ball. "If you want to play with it, you have to pay me three hundred rupees," Bashir said, sipping his remaining tea.

Katib looked at his mother. She offered no help.

"How do I pay three hundred rupees? I have no money."

"I don't know, you tell me." Bashir straightened up, smoothed the wrinkles on his Kameez, and walked to the tap near the door to wash up. "If you want to be a cricketer, you must practice a lot. The sooner you start, the better. But you can't start practicing until you pay me."

Katib took a moment to ponder.

"I can give you half of my daily earnings," he proposed.

"You won't earn much from shoe shining," Bashir countered. "And I can't afford to wait too long for my payment."

Katib considered before suggesting, "I'll offer shoe shining near Haq Plaza. I have seen rich men come there. They have shoes that need polishing. And I'll charge them more because they can afford it."

Bashir smiled momentarily, but upon turning to Katib, he replaced it with a grave expression.

"Okay. You can play with it now," Bashir approved.

Katib grinned, seized the bat, and launched the ball into the sky. As gravity pulled it down, he struck it forcefully with the tip of the cricket bat, sending it soaring back upward.

Katib couldn't wait to go out and show off his brand-new cricket kit to the neighborhood boys. He had already decided who'd be allowed on his team and who would sit on the stairs and only watch. He wished he could share it with Gul Khan. All he remembered was that they placed his body in a bag and zipped it. *Maybe they'll take him to his mother.* A comforting thought crossed Katib's mind. *He needs to go home.*

Outside, the sky was clear—a beautiful sunny day. On the streets, rickshaws roared, and the shopkeepers opened their shops while chatting about the recent ODI.

As Bashir mounted his bicycle, ready to depart for work, he paused, turning to Rukhsana. "Listen, if you want to leave, maybe live with your parents, you can go. I'll be fine."

Rukhsana placed her hand on his arm. "You are not just Kareem's brother; you are my brother too. And this is my home," she smiled.

Bashir couldn't help but smile back.

When he left the house, he saw a man waiting for him across the street, next to a rickshaw. As soon as he saw Bashir, he immediately approached him.

"Can I help you?" Bashir asked, bringing his bicycle to an immediate halt.

"Are you Bashir Ali?" The man held out his hand to shake Bashir's.

Bashir shook his hand. "Yes," he replied.

"I am Saadat, Kareem's friend," the man said. "I am sorry for your loss," he added, shaking his head in disbelief. "This is very tragic. I haven't been able to sleep since I heard about Kareem."

"Thank you for coming here," Bashir said, trying to conceal

his emotions.

"I didn't just come to offer my condolences," the man said.

"Did he owe you money too?" Bashir asked anxiously.

"No, no." The man waved his hands. "I came to give you this." He pointed at the rickshaw standing nearby.

"Kareem bought this from me. He asked me to paint it," he said. "I didn't know he would not be here to ride it."

Bashir looked at the new rickshaw, and the barrier holding off the flood of tears broke loose. He hid his face in his shoulder scarf, mourning the loss. The man patted Bashir's shoulder, then left quietly. Bashir sobbed into his shoulder scarf longer than he could remember ever having done before. He no longer had to worry about the debt.

* * *

With his brand new bat and ball, Katib approached the neighborhood children playing cricket in an empty alley. They saw him but ignored him as always.

This time, he made no requests to join the team. Instead, he tossed the ball high, making them turn their heads and look up. The ball went above the rooftops, almost as if it had wings. The boys abandoned their game to watch it soar and then come blazing down, only to be forced back up by Katib's cricket bat.

*** The End ***

www.ingramcontent.com/pod-product-compliance
Lightning Source LLC
Chambersburg PA
CBHW070337130626
46556CB00007B/2898